THE W

After all that had happened to her in the past few months, Simon Egan was a balm to Meg `Somers'' feelings. She started to dare to lift her face to the sun again and find happiness—sure that her winter was behind her . . .

Books you will enjoy
by LILLIAN CHEATHAM

SHADOWED REUNION

When her marriage to Sacha Kimberly broke up, Katie had thought Hawaii was far enough away for her to run from him—and to conceal the fact that she had had his child. Now, after five years, Sacha had caught up with her. And if she didn't agree to his suggestion he was going to take the child away from her...

THE ISLAND OF DOLPHINS

Juliet arrived in the Caribbean expecting to help Mark Bannerman work on his book about dolphins, but instead found his brother James there... which began a whole set of problems for her.

LADY WITH A PAST

Josey had a past she didn't want Thorne to know about. But when Thorne was the man who was involved in it, and was also now her husband, how could she prevent him from finding out about it? And when he did, where would that leave her?

THE WINTER HEART

BY

LILLIAN CHEATHAM

MILLS & BOON LIMITED
15–16 BROOK'S MEWS
LONDON W1A 1DR

All the characters in this book have no existence outside the imagination of the Author, and have no relation whatsoever to anyone bearing the same name or names. They are not even distantly inspired by any individual known or unknown to the Author, and all the incidents are pure invention.

The text of this publication or any part thereof may not be reproduced or transmitted in any form or by any means, electronic or mechanical, including photocopying, recording, storage in an information retrieval system, or otherwise, without the written permission of the publisher.

This book is sold subject to the condition that it shall not, by way of trade or otherwise, be lent, resold, hired out or otherwise circulated without the prior consent of the publisher in any form of binding or cover other than that in which it is published and without a similar condition including this condition being imposed on the subsequent purchaser.

*First published in Great Britain 1985
by Mills & Boon Limited*

© Lillian Cheatham 1985

*Australian copyright 1985
Philippine copyright 1986
This edition 1986*

ISBN 0 263 75276 3

*Set in Monophoto Times 10 on 10½ pt.
01-0286 – 57412*

*Made and printed in Great Britain by
Richard Clay (The Chaucer Press) Ltd,
Bungay, Suffolk*

CHAPTER ONE

MEG Somers manoeuvred the key into the lock with her arms full while pushing open the door with her hip. It was late, for she had stopped at the all-night market on her way home. The car in which she had ridden gave a faint toot before pulling away from the kerb. The driver was her boss, Pierre Frontand, the owner of the restaurant where she worked split hours at lunch and dinner time. She was seldom home before midnight when she rode with Pierre.

The lights were on all over the little apartment but Meg knew it was empty even before she walked in. It had the feel of emptiness, quite apart from the lack of noise from Carol's never-ending radio music. There was a smell of stale cigarette smoke, too, but no blue drift of smoke quivering on the air currents—another sign of Carol's absence.

On her way to the bedroom, she glanced into Carol's room. It was a disaster. Discarded clothes were strewn across the bed, indicating that Carol had had trouble making her selection for tonight. Meg couldn't tell from her crowded wardrobe what her final choice had been.

She picked up wet towels and tidied the counter in the bathroom before showering and slipping into a flimsy nightgown and matching shorty robe. At her dressing-table mirror, she loosened her hair from its daytime confinement and began her ritual nightly brushing. In southern Florida, even in early spring, the nights were warm, and just about any breeze held a scent of the sea.

Ordinarily, the act of brushing her hair calmed Meg but tonight, sleep was the last thing on her mind. She frowned, then reminded herself that frowns brought wrinkles and God knows, at twenty-four, she didn't need any more of those. Meg Somers was too thin and angular for conventional prettiness, but she always looked marvellous in whatever she wore and her eyes were a remarkable green, as changeable as the sea. Her dark red hair and high cheekbones, plus a natural elegance, gave her an air of distinction that was an asset in her job, which was as hostess at a rather famous French restaurant. She was well liked by her co-workers and most of the pampered, well-fed customers knew her as a decorative part of the décor.

She could have been a model but since no one ever told her that, she assumed that the real beauty of the family was her eighteen-year-old stepsister, Carol. So did Carol, who never failed to remind Meg that *her* hair did not turn carrot red in the sun, and *she* did not have a crop of freckles every summer. Instead, Carol's hair was red gold, and her figure curved in all the right places. Her wide blue eyes could melt with innocence and she had a golden tan. And ever since Carol had been old enough to look into a mirror, she had known she was destined for stardom.

Thinking about Carol and where she was right now increased Meg's restlessness and she rose abruptly and went into the kitchen, snapping off lights on the way. The apartment wasn't large—besides the two bedrooms, bath and kitchen, there was only the living-room with a dining alcove for four. All the furniture in it belonged to Meg's mother. The apartment, one half a duplex bungalow, had been the best Meg's stepmother could find when they had had to move after Arnold Somers' death. The kitchen was the brightest room in the place, with its row of African violets on the window sill and the bright yellow face of the happy day clock. Meg glanced at it again. Right now, the hands stood at one-thirty. Where was Carol? She had always been difficult to control but lately, she had been much worse—since that job of hers, in fact. Besides staying out late most nights, she refused to discuss her new lover, for Carol had admitted he was that. He dropped her off and sped away at night, and Meg was never at home to meet him when he picked Carol up. Just thinking of the possibilities made Meg's stomach knot with tension and she poured herself a glass of milk to settle her incipient ulcer. Wondering about Carol and where she could be at this time of night made her realise how little she really knew about her stepsister. That had been brought home last winter, when the police called her down to the station house to inform her that Carol had been picked up on a charge of shoplifting.

It had been the school counsellor who suggested that Carol get an after-school job so she could have money to buy the things she craved. And Meg saw that it would keep her occupied while she was working. But the job had signalled the beginning of the real change in Carol. Late hours, secretiveness, sullen resentment when questioned and then, last week, her vicious anger when Meg called her employers. Meg had been half crazy that night, sitting up waiting for her, when she 'phoned the Hardwicks. She had thought Carol worked for them as a babysitter, and the address had been in one of Miami's wealthier neighbourhoods. But the maid who answered the 'phone stated positively that no one by the name of Carol Smith worked there.

Carol had been furious when she learned about it. 'How dare you call around asking questions about me?' she had screamed. 'Are you trying to make me lose my job?'

'What job?' Meg demanded. 'It's certainly not with the Hardwicks! Carol, you lied to me. You told me you took care of the Hardwicks' children! I demand to know the truth, or I'll go to the school counsellor. She's more or less responsible to the police for you.'

Carol's rage cooled in a hurry with that. 'All right, all right, keep your shirt on,' she muttered. 'I do work for the Hardwicks. If you don't believe me, you can call Mr Hardwick at his office. Mrs Hardwick has been sick, and that was one of the nurses. She doesn't know who I am. But, damn it, Meg, I mean it! I won't have you checking on me with the people I work for. They'll think there's something queer about me if my sister starts asking questions of them.'

'Surely they know that as an eighteen-year-old, they are partly responsible for——'

Carol glared at her. 'No one is responsible for me but myself!' she snapped. 'I look after myself.'

'*I* look after you, Carol,' Meg said firmly. 'And I wouldn't be doing my duty if I didn't find out about this boy you've been dating——'

'*Boy!*' Carol threw back her head and laughed. 'Don't be naïve! He's a man. God, Meg, you're simple! I don't date boys—they can't give me what I want. They don't know how to make love for one thing, and they're usually broke, and they're just about as subtle as a bull in a china shop. I've found a man who meets my requirements—and he has money!'

'You're too young!' Meg cried. 'Does he know how old you are? What sort of man would go with an eighteen-year-old high-school student——'

'My sort.' Carol smile tauntingly and rose from the table. She and Meg had been eating breakfast—it was the only hour of the day they had together—and Carol turned and started out the door. 'Sorry, Meg, but I've got to rush. It's time for school.'

'I'm not through!' Meg gripped her arm. She was disturbed and confused by Carol's revelations. The girl had always been a problem, but until lately, Meg had been able to control her. 'I don't intend to let you get involved with a man who is taking advantage of your age and inexperience——'

Carol laughed. 'Inexperience? Wise up, Meg. You can't stop me. You're not related to me. In fact, you're not even a friend!' she added contemptuously.

Meg flinched. 'Until you finish school, I'm your legal guardian.'

'That's a lie!' Carol flashed triumphantly. 'After Mom died, instead of telling the social worker that I was your stepsister, you pretended we were real sisters. I heard about the whole thing from Mrs McNeely. She came home from the hospital talking about my sweet, generous stepsister, who wanted to keep me with her so badly she'd lied her head off to the social worker. But there was nothing *legal* about it! No one asked me if I'd rather be adopted! They just listened to you. Well, I'm eighteen now, and I want to live my life! I want to go places—Hollywood—New York! I want to get out of this dump!' She looked around the small, shabby kitchen scathingly.

It wasn't the first time Carol had complained about the way she lived but Meg hadn't realised her resentment was so great. It was especially ironical in view of the fact that Meg had lied to the social worker because of her stepmother's dying request that she make a home for Carol.

'I'm sorry you feel that way about it,' she said stiffly.

'Meg, for years I've listened to you trying to turn me into another dull, plodding workaholic like you! Well, I have news for you, Meg. I can't think of anything more deadly than to be like you! I'd be a lot better off leaving school and concentrating on my acting and modelling! What good will school do me in Hollywood? So, just stay off my back!'

That had been last week and for a few days, Carol had seemed better, as though Meg, by easing up on her, had made her more thoughtful about coming in earlier at night. Meg had hoped it meant Carol was snapping out of her grandiose Hollywood schemes. God knows, she didn't need the aggravation, Meg reflected bleakly. The doctor had warned her about a possible ulcer when she had been so ill a year ago, and advised her bluntly to do something about Carol.

'Don't you know it takes two parents to raise an overactive teenager these days, and you've been going it alone since you were seventeen. When did *you* last go to a party, or buy a new dress for yourself? This is your body's way of rebelling against the extra demands you've put on it.'

All of which, though true, did not change the habits of a lifetime—or nearly a lifetime, ever since Alice Smith married Meg's father, Arnold Somers, and eight-year-old Meg fell in love with her new stepmother and pretty little two-year-old stepsister. Alice easily slipped into the role of her own mother, who had been dead for several years.

When Meg was thirteen, her father died and Alice assumed responsibility for Meg. No relatives stepped forward to offer to take the child and so, together, they took over the task of spoiling Carol, who was a little beauty. Alice naïvely felt that Carol's beauty made her special, and although at times she felt a little guilty about the sacrifices Meg had to make, she felt comfortably certain they were united in their ambitions for Carol. When Meg was seventeen, Alice was killed in an accident at an intersection. Meg was driving their elderly car but the other driver ran through a stop light. Alice died in Meg's arms, her last words a plea for Meg to keep Carol. It meant giving up her scholarship to art school, her hopes for the future, and getting a job as a waitress to support them, but Meg did it gladly, without hesitation.

But, apparently, Carol resented those years, the sacrifices she had made, the poverty, the lack of small luxuries that Alice had been able to provide. She felt that Meg had denied her a chance to be adopted by wealthy parents by keeping her. It was a fantasy, of

THE WINTER HEART

course, but one she continued to cling to, and no amount of reasoned argument or explanations by Meg had made her change her mind. And, now, she had begun to claim that Meg's motive had been jealousy and envy of her beauty.

With a sigh, Meg rose and rinsed her glass then switched off the light and started towards her bedroom. She was confident in the dark—she knew every inch of the little apartment. As she reached the living-room, she was startled by a loud knock on the front door. Through the uncurtained window, she could see by the street light that there were no cars parked outside. She hesitated, then the knock came again and this time, she head Carol, sobbing with terror.

'Meg! Meg! For God's sake, let me in!'

Meg ran forward and fumbled with the night latch, then flung the door open.

'Why didn't you use your key?'

'I—I di-didn't have it!' Carol stumbled into the room, then closed the door and began frantically snapping the locks.

Meg pulled the curtains then switched on the light. Carol flung her arm up to shield her face, and Meg saw that it was covered with a long, bloody scrape from elbow to palm. There was another scrape on her leg, and her dress was torn and covered with blood and dirt. Meg pulled her hand down and looked at her face. It was bruised and swollen, as though she had been crying a long time.

'My God, Carol, what happened?' she breathed, but she sickly knew.

Carol stumbled over to the couch and flung herself down. It was a moment or two before she spoke. 'Oh, Meg, you were so right!'

Meg put a pillow behind her head, then ran into the kitchen for some water. 'Here, drink this. What happened to you?'

Carol drank obediently, holding the glass between shaking hands like a child. Meg vaguely sensed that Carol's brain was busy behind her innocent eyes, making up a story, and she felt slightly impatient. Did Carol think she would *blame* her for having got into a situation where she was raped? She promised herself grimly that the man responsible was going to be made to pay for this.

Carol began to cry again, and her tears weren't very pretty. Meg went to the bathroom and brought back a bowl of water and a washcloth. She began to wash her face and some of the blood off her arm and leg. The pain brought Carol out of her crying fit, and she sat up abruptly and pulled at Meg's hand.

'Leave that, Meg! I have to talk to you—at once!'

'All right, talk away.'

Carol ripped a tissue from the box on the coffee table and blew her nose. 'Oh, Meg, you were so right. You—you warned me b-but I didn't listen. I was wrong, Meg, I know that now.'

'Darling, I'm sorry.' She put her arm around Carol. 'Do you want to tell me what happened, or would you rather not talk about it just yet?' When Carol merely stared at her in a dazed, uncomprehending way, she added, 'Where did it happen?'

'On a bad curve near the Hardwick home. The road goes around a lake, and it's easy to miss in the dark. I—we—had just left the house——'

'We?'

'Tony Hardwick and I. He—he was bringing me home.'

'Was he the one?' Meg asked fiercely. 'Was he the one who raped you?'

'*Raped* me?' Carol sounded horrified. 'Meg, he's *dead*! And—I'm so scared!'

'Dead? You mean you killed him!'

Carol paled. 'Don't say that!' she wailed. 'It was an

accident! T-Tony was driving, I swear it, Meg! The car wasn't going that fast b-but it just seemed to—to leap into the air! Tony and I were b-both thrown out, but I landed clear and—and Tony landed on his head! It was so bloody and—oh, God, Meg, I was so scared!'

'Do you mean you were in a *car wreck*?'

'Honestly, Meg, it wasn't my fault,' Carol sobbed. 'It was like the time you were driving and Mom was killed. I never blamed you for that! You said it wasn't your fault and I believed you! Remember?' She raised wide, innocent eyes, drenched with tears and blue as cornflowers, and Meg wondered if even in the midst of her panic, she could be so devious as to remind her that she had been the one to make her an orphan, and therefore, owed her something, even if it was just a belief in her innocence. '*I* wasn't driving,' Carol added childishly. Meg, already alerted, knew she was lying. 'Tony was driving but he wasn't going fast. But it was late—and h-he *had* been drinking and——'

'If you weren't driving, then you have nothing to worry about,' Meg said shortly. She wondered if it could be proved who was driving, for Carol didn't have a licence. 'What did the police say about it?'

Carol burst into tears and began to babble incoherently. Meg soon gathered that the police had not been called. Instead, Carol had run and kept on running until she got home.

'That was stupid!' Meg snapped. 'What if he wasn't dead?'

'Oh, but he was. He had to be! No one could live—after *that*!' Carol shuddered.

'Well, it will have to be reported now.' Meg put her hand on the 'phone. 'Let's just hope someone else has found the wreck and you aren't charged with negligence.'

'No, don't call!' Carol clutched her arm feverishly. 'Don't, Meg! Keep me out of it!'

'How can I keep you out of it? Did anyone see you with this Tony? You don't have your handbag—where is it? Did you leave it there?'

Carol looked stunned, and Meg picked up the 'phone. This time, Carol didn't try to stop her.

The sergeant at the police station was very polite and said he would send someone out to speak to her sister as soon as a man could be spared. The accident had been discovered but he knew none of the details, he said, except that Tony Hardwick was definitely dead. Meg got the impression from his voice that he was hiding something from her.

'I knew it!' Carol cried hysterically. 'They're going to put all the blame on me, just because of that other thing—that shoplifting! Meg, you can't let them do it! You told Mom you'd look after me, and so far, you've done a rotten job of it! Tonight, you destroyed me! I *told* you not to call the police!'

Meg tried to soothe her but there was no calming Carol now.

'It's because I have a record! Can't you understand *anything*?' Her hands twisted in her lap. 'I'm listed on the police blotter as a criminal. Do you think the rich Hardwick family is going to let it be said that their precious Tony was driving, when they can blame it on a defenceless girl? Someone who was a *servant*? They'll say I was driving and I'll get all the blame! Oh, Meg,' she added wildly, 'you're a fool! You believe the police are always right, and an innocent citizen never gets blamed! You're so—so *stupid*!'

Meg shifted uncomfortably. Was Carol right? Was she a fool? Would they blame Carol because of her record? Perhaps they might say she was drinking, and Meg suspected she had been. In that case, they might send Carol to prison.

'I'm sorry,' she faltered. 'I thought it was for the best.' As Carol's sobs increased, she added apologetically, 'You know I'd do anything I could to help you, honey, but——'

Carol seized on that phrase as though she had been waiting for it. 'Will you? Do you really mean that, Meg? Would you do anything to help me? Oh, please, say you mean it, Meg! Please, please, say *you* were in the accident!' She was shaking all over. 'It would be all right then, because you haven't a record. It wouldn't matter if you said you were the one with Tony.'

'Carol, that—that's crazy!' Meg was horrified. 'How can I possibly claim I was in the car with a man I never saw before? I don't know anything about him or what happened——'

'I can tell you!' Carol interrupted feverishly. 'I can tell you everything you need to know about him and the accident—and everything! It'll be easy to carry it off. You'll see! Oh, Meg, please say you'll do it. You—you *owe* it to me!'

In vain, Meg tried to reason with Carol, but she was beyond all reason. She was wild with determination and possessed of one driving aim—to force Meg to agree to the impersonation. She argued, pleaded, stormed, cried, and over and over, threatened that if Meg *really* loved her, she would do this one thing to keep her out of prison. By this time, Meg had her back to the wall. Once, she tried to point out that the Hardwicks would not be fooled by an imposter, but Carol brushed that objection aside.

'You won't be meeting any of the Hardwicks, and as for the rest, it will be all right because I used your name when I applied for the job. Because of having a record, you see. I took your social security number. Everyone at the Hardwick house knew me as Meg Somers. That's why the maid said she didn't know Carol Smith.' She was apparently oblivious to Meg's surprise and distaste. Her teeth chattered and her eyes were demented. 'Remember Mom, Meg! You promised her, remember?

You owe it to her! And, if you do this one last thing for me, I'll never give you a moment's worry again! I—I'll be *so* good, Meg!'

Finally, Meg gave in. She met the policemen who came out an hour later and told them she was the other occupant of the car. They accepted it, for they already had been given her name as being Tony Hardwick's companion on his last ride. They were courteous and soothing, even when Meg refused to sign a statement about the accident, but she didn't think they believed her story that she couldn't remember a thing from the time she got into the car until she arrived home. However, since it was not a criminal matter, they were obliged to accept her explanation. It was the one point on which she had stood firm with Carol. She would not put her name to a perjured statement, nor would she appear in court and lie. She knew that her stepsister was listening, frantic with fear, behind the door while she talked to the policemen, and Meg found herself hoping they would give her a loophole by demanding that she sign a statement.

But there was no problem. As they were leaving, Meg stopped the older policeman with a question that had been worrying her. 'How is the Hardwick family taking this, Officer?'

He looked at her disapprovingly. 'Mrs Hardwick is taking it mighty bad, ma'am. I expect you understand that under the circumstances, we called out the doctor before we told her her husband was dead.' He closed the door gently behind him.

'Why didn't you tell me he was married?' she demanded of Carol, who stumbled out from behind the door as soon as the policemen were gone.

'What does it matter?' Carol asked impatiently. 'They were separated. They had one of those arrangements that people have.'

'Arrangements?'

'They didn't sleep together. They just lived in the same house. That's the way people with money do when they don't want to divide the money, or they can't come to terms on community property and that sort of thing,' Carol added vaguely.

'And just how do *you* know about their sleeping arrangements?' Meg demanded harshly.

'I worked there, remember. Tony had his suite of rooms and his wife had hers.'

'And the children?' When Carol looked blank, Meg added sardonically, 'You do remember the children, don't you? The ones you were hired to take care of?'

'Oh, there weren't any children.' Carol's vagueness increased. 'I was supposed to be a sort of companion to Barbara, Tony's wife. She has—had been ill and needed a sort of—of nurse. Mostly just for things like helping her dress and bringing her trays. But she was so bitchy and ordered me around like I was dirt, that I finally couldn't take it any longer and I quit a couple of days ago.'

Meg took all that with a grain of salt. None of it rang true, but it hardly seemed worth arguing about now. 'Anyway,' she said, 'she must have felt something for her husband because the policeman said she was taking it hard.'

'All an act,' Carol sniped viciously. 'She likes for everyone to feel sorry for her. She's good at getting sympathy—that's how she kept Tony. She played that so-called illness of hers for all it was worth, trying to make him feel guilty every time he walked out of the house without her!'

Meg didn't bother to reply. Learning that Tony Hardwick was married was a shock, and she wondered what other lies Carol had told her. She had changed a lot from that sweet little girl Mom had loved. Meg didn't even know her anymore, but she had already decided that the next time Carol offered to leave, she would give her blessing without a demur. She didn't owe Carol a thing any longer, not even a worn out promise to Mom.

The details of the accident were given in a skimpy report on the back page of the local newspaper. Meg's name was not even mentioned. The obituary notice gave Anthony Hardwick's age as thirty-two, and his wife as his only surviving relative. Meg, reading the notice, wished she could extend her sympathy to the widow, but of course, it wouldn't do. If she was grieving, Barbara Melton Hardwick would not appreciate a visit from the sister of her recent employee. If she was vengeful towards Carol, it would be dangerous, and if she didn't know about her, it would be foolish. Under the circumstances, it would be better to do nothing.

The following day, a lawyer visited Meg with a waiver from the insurance company, which she steadfastly refused to sign. She saw the lawyer was suspicious and so she agreed to see a doctor of his choosing and allow him to sign a medical waiver.

That seemed the end of it until a few days later, when the storm broke.

Meg saw the photographs on the front page when she brought in the morning paper. There were two of them, one of a sad-eyed blonde and the other a handsome man with a facile, charming smile. The headline read: 'Grieving Widow Takes Own Life'. That was followed with 'Grieving over the accidental death of her husband, heiress Barbara Melton Hardwick took her own life after learning of his involvement with her pretty nurse-companion. The body was discovered yesterday afternoon by her lawyer, Charles Shaw, when he became suspicious after . . .'

Meg moaned, 'God, no!' She read on, growing more shocked as the story unfolded. Apparently, Barbara Hardwick had committed suicide after leaving notes for her brother and the police in which she said that she did not want to live, with her husband dead, and knowing that he had betrayed her with her former nurse companion, Margaret Somers. Meg sucked in her breath protestingly. The manner in which Barbara Hardwick performed her own execution would surely grip the imagination of the public.

Barbara had been a diabetic, dependent upon daily insulin injections to keep alive. She was madly in love with her husband, and totally dependent upon him. In her anguish and disillusionment, she had dismissed all her servants and given herself an overdose of insulin.

Apparently, Barbara's parents were dead and her only survivor was a brother, who was somewhere in South America. Her lawyer, who had been the spokesman for the news items, added that his client had told him she was closing up her house to go and stay with friends, and it wasn't until he met one of those friends this morning that he had become suspicious and investigated. He added that his client blamed the woman, Margaret Somers, for her husband's death, since she firmly believed she was driving at the time of the accident.

Just then, the 'phone shrilled and Meg picked it up, although the last thing she wanted to do right now was talk to anyone. The female voice at the other end of the line was briskly cheerful. 'Miss Somers?'

'Yes,' Meg said cautiously.

'Miss Margaret Somers?'

'Yes. Who is this, please?'

'This is the *Daily News*, Miss Somers. I would like your reaction to the death of Mrs Barbara Hardwick.'

Meg choked. 'How dare you call me about that!'

'Now, Miss Somers, I suggest you co-operate with the press. You're going to need all the good publicity you can get. Everyone is going to be interested in knowing how you feel about her suicide. For instance, were you and Tony Hardwick running away when the accident occurred? May I quote you to our readers as saying that you now feel guilt and remorse——'

Meg slammed down the 'phone.

'Who was that?' Carol was standing in the doorway, yawning.

Meg told her, vindictively pleased to see Carol react to the news by turning pale. But it was fright, not remorse that had shocked her, and her fear soon made her take out her spite on Barbara Hardwick.

'That dirty bitch! She did it on purpose—to ruin me! She knew Tony loved me. He despised her. He only married her because of her money and she hung on to him with her whining and pleading, when she knew he loved me! Oh! Oh, how I hate her for doing this! She used her illness to make him feel guilty. To keep him! Wasn't that awful, Meg? Can you blame me for hating her? For—for feeling she wasn't fair to keep Tony's money——'

'I thought you said it was her money,' Meg interrupted grimly.

'Well, maybe it was,' Carol admitted sullenly. 'But he deserved something for just having to live with her. He would've married me, I know he would've, but she wouldn't let him go. She hung on. She refused—it was all her fault—she was to blame, not me! That's why she killed herself! Because she knew she caused it all!'

Meg was shocked by Carol's insensitivity to Barbara Hardwick's pain. She still did not see what she had put the other woman through. Whether Tony loved her or not, didn't matter—why hadn't she understood what she was doing to Barbara? Meg wondered if it had been her fault—had she turned Carol into this by her constant catering to her whims? Or was it something in Carol herself, in the genes inherited from the father who deserted Alice before their daughter was born? Not that it mattered, for her character had been formed too long now for Meg to try to change her.

By noon, they were in a state of siege. The curtains were drawn, and they were not answering the doorbell or telephone. At three o'clock, Meg called her boss, Pierre Frontand. As soon as he heard her voice, he said worriedly, 'Meg, what's going on? I have reporters all over the place waiting for you so they can ask you some questions about a strange woman who committed suicide.'

'Do you—will you want me to come to work tonight?' she faltered.

'God, *no*!' He sounded horrified. 'But we have to talk. I'll come over there after I close the restaurant tonight.'

He appeared promptly at midnight. By then, the reporters had given up for the night, and he was able to get in without any trouble. He followed Meg straight through to the kitchen, where she offered him coffee.

'What's this all about, Meg?' Pierre was a handsome Frenchman of about forty, whose charm was lavished on the patrons of his restaurant. Otherwise, he was a hard taskmaster. About a month ago, he had asked Meg to marry him, confessing frankly that it was more or less a business proposition. Now, he was looking angry and tense, and she knew he was afraid the scandal was going to recoil on his restaurant. 'I happen to know you did not work for that Hardwick woman, nor could you have been in that wreck. I tried to tell the reporters, but they won't believe me unless you deny the whole thing. Why haven't you done it, yet?'

Meg explained. Pierre knew about the shoplifting, since he had been in the office when the police called.

'Are you serious?' he demanded, frankly astounded. 'Are you really going to take the blame for the mess that little delinquent cooked up?'

Meg sighed and pushed a hand through her unkempt

hair. She hadn't had a chance to brush it in its usual smooth coil this morning, and she knew from Pierre's expression that she was looking terrible. She felt sore, bruised, tired, and she wished Pierre would stop glaring at her and take her into his arms. 'I can't let the police question her, Pierre,' she explained wearily, again. 'I'm pretty sure she was driving and I know she was drinking. If they find out, they'll throw the book at her. She hasn't got a licence, you know.'

He studied her frowningly. 'Then you're a fool,' he said heavily. 'If you refuse to set the record straight, I'll have to assume you don't wish to continue working for me, because, frankly, I can't afford the bad publicity. In fact, if you don't speak out and clear the good name of the restaurant, I shall question your loyalty to me and our mutual interests.'

He left shortly after that, scowling at Carol who was curled on the couch, using the telephone. Meg felt sick at the quick, ruthless way he had cut her off. She had worked for him since she was seventeen. She knew the restaurant was all-important to him, but he *had* asked her to marry him, and she thought he felt something for her. He knew she wasn't guilty, either. She closed the door sadly behind him, knowing this spelled the end to one part of her life.

Carol was still on the telephone when she went to bed, a Carol who smiled guiltily at her. The next morning, Meg rose early after a sleepless night, and found her stepsister already in the kitchen, fresh and dewy in her baby doll pyjamas and bare feet.

'Are you going to try to get another job?' she asked casually.

'I guess so,' Meg said shortly. 'Somebody has to.'

'That's what I mean,' Carol said sweetly. 'I didn't want you to have to worry about me. I'll be moving out this morning.' She placed a slice of bread in the toaster. 'I thought it would take the pressure off you if I went.'

'Pressure?'

'Of having to support me. Now, you can do something for yourself, Meg. Go back to school—or something.'

'Go back to school? At twenty-four?' Meg asked incredulously.

Carol flushed defensively. 'Well, it was just a thought.' She sounded injured. 'You needn't bite my head off! I thought you'd welcome the chance to be on your own.'

Meg said nothing but apparently her silence stirred Carol's conscience for she added guiltily, 'All right, Meg, I admit it! I'm a pig to ditch you like this, but I—I just can't take it! All this business about Tony is getting to me. And I'm scared you're going to break down and talk.' She sounded half defiant, half ashamed. 'I heard your boss saying last night you should. Are—are you, Meg?'

'No,' Meg said coldly.

'Gee, thanks! I—I didn't think you would but I just can't take the chance. Anyway, I called a friend while you were talking to your boss last night and asked him to pick me up. He'll be here in about an hour.'

'Fine,' Meg said calmly. 'Don't make it any later, please. I need to make some plans, too.'

Carol looked disconcerted. 'Wha-what are you going to do?'

'I really don't think that's any of your business, do you?' Meg inquired sweetly. 'That last call was from the *Enquirer*, and with them on my trail, I think I'd better beat a retreat, don't you?'

'I guess so,' Carol muttered.

Her pick-up was a sleazy youth who pulled up in a dented, rusted Thunderbird and tooted his horn at the kerb. Carol came out of her bedroom, carrying two of the best suitcases in the house.

'I guess I'll be going now. That's Kit.' She looked at Meg expectantly. 'All this furniture and stuff? Er—are you going to sell it?'

'Probably,' Meg said coolly.

'I guess the money should be yours,' Carol said reluctantly. 'It belonged to your mother.'

'I guess you're right.' Meg looked at the girl she had loved and cherished most of her life. 'Goodbye, Carol. I hope you get everything that's coming to you.'

'Ready, baby?' It was Kit. 'What gives?' he added, taking one of the suitcases.

Carol said something in a low voice and they went down the front steps. The last Meg saw of the Thunderbird as it turned the corner was a brief flash of colour from the plastic streamers tied to the radio antenna.

Meg had sold the furniture by noon by simply calling all the second-hand dealers in the 'phone book until she found one who would buy the whole lot. It was to be picked up early the next morning. That afternoon, she cleaned the house, ruthlessly disposing of everything that could not be packed into one suitcase. The next morning, the movers were in and out in one hour. After they were through, Meg called a cab, stopped at the bank and closed her account, dropped off her key at the real estate office, then went on to the bus station.

An hour later, she was on the first express headed north. The sign on it said Jacksonville, but she wasn't particular. She wasn't leaving anyone behind she cared about.

CHAPTER TWO

IN Jacksonville, Meg checked into a quiet, cheap motel that offered special rates and one-room efficiency apartments. She fell into bed and slept for twelve hours straight, and when she awakened, she rolled over and gazed at the ceiling as she pondered her future plans. She had figured out what she wanted to do on the bus coming up here. Carol's suggestion had stuck in her mind. Why not go to art school? It had been the career she wanted when Mom's death cut it short. But had her talent dried up on her? And would her savings last through art school *and* the lean years while she was trying to sell her work? She didn't think so.

She would have to support herself. What she needed was some training that would result in a part-time job, yet allow her the time and energy to continue with her art.

She rose and dressed and then, after enquiring of the desk clerk, caught a city bus to a business school that was part of a national chain and had the reputation for finding good jobs for its graduates. Fortunately, a new term was just beginning that morning, and she registered for a full series of courses. On the way home, she stopped at an art store and purchased supplies. She wouldn't have time to paint much until she finished school, but she was anxious to see if she still could. What she ended up with was a glowing burst of colour that literally sang on the canvas, and expressed in vivid fashion Meg's present feelings.

The next morning, she began school, the beginning of a long, hot summer which she spent mostly indoors, studying before a humming, chattering air conditioner.

Occasionally, in idle moments, she painted, but her energies were mostly concentrated on coming out well in the overload of courses she was taking. At the end of the summer, she graduated with honours, at the top of her class, and with a promise from Helen Rogers, the careers adviser, to find her the kind of job she was looking for.

On the last day of school, Helen stopped her in the hallway.

'Something unusual has just come up,' she told Meg. 'I thought of you at once because the man said he didn't want the usual run of silly young girls to apply. The only trouble is the job is full-time, but it's temporary—three months at the most—and the salary is unusually good.' She named it. 'Are you interested?'

Meg whistled. 'At that salary! Of course I am!'

'Come on into the office and I'll tell you about it.'

'Have you ever heard of Simon Egan?' she asked when she and Meg were seated across the desk from one another.

Meg's eyes widened. 'The writer?' Helen nodded. 'Who hasn't?'

Helen smiled. 'Ninety per cent of our graduates.' She was a pleasant widow of about fifty and she had no illusions about the teenagers the school turned out. Meg was something else. Helen knew about her art ambitions and she wanted to help her. Helen sensed a mystery about her, but Meg was reticent, and Helen liked that. 'I am sure most of them have seen some of his movies or television plays, even if they haven't read his books. Well, he's in our city, believe it or not, and he wants a typist to help him while he's researching some material for a new book. It will be a great recommendation for your next job. Interested?'

'Naturally. But, surely he has a secretary?'

Helen shrugged. 'He says not. His own typing is strictly two-finger method, and he usually has his manuscripts typed professionally. But while he's here, he's rushed for time and wants someone who can take his scrawled handwritten notes and transcribe them. And with that salary he is offering, you can afford to take a couple of months off afterwards to look for the kind of part-time job you want.'

'Yes, you're right.'

'There is one catch. You may be required to work at night occasionally. He lives in one of those big apartment hotels at the beach. Didn't you tell me you intended moving out of that place where you're staying now?'

'Yes.'

'Right now, the off-season rates make it cheap to live at the beach. If you get the job, I can help you find a place near his that you can afford.'

'Thanks, Helen.'

'Don't thank me yet until you've seen if you like him. I made an appointment for an interview and after that, you're on your own. He sounded like he knew what he wanted and, of course, he can afford to pay for it. I just hope he isn't too dictatorial for you.'

Meg grinned. 'At the salary he's paying, he can be as bossy as he likes.'

Meg dipped into her slender savings to buy a new dress for the interview, a creamy jersey with a wide bronze belt that showed off her slim waist. With a new lipstick, a glossy cocoa that gave her mouth a tawny look, and her red hair brushed into a smooth coil at the nape of her neck, she looked like a really confident woman. She wanted to look attractive, yet dignified, hopefully the kind of girl a man like Simon Egan would appreciate and want as his secretary.

Approaching the luxurious ocean-front hotel from the bus stop, she noted the presence of a doorman who took her name and used the house telephone before sending her up by lift to Mr Egan's suite on the top floor. After her experience with the press, Meg could appreciate his desire to retain his privacy. A man who turned out a bestseller a year and whose books were snapped up and made into successful movies or television plays as soon as they were in print, would have a healthy respect for the snooping capabilities of the press, not to mention that of the groupies and hangers-on who tried to get close to famous men.

She tried to remember what she had read about him, which wasn't much since he seemed to be able to keep his personal life very personal. She was an avid reader of his books, and thought she could guess something of the kind of man he was from that. His plots were well constructed, tautly thrilling adventure tales that kept you glued to the book until the last page. It was said he researched them himself, travelling to places like Africa or the polar regions for his locales. Women played a minor role in his books, and Meg suspected that he was rather chauvinistic in his attitude towards her sex, perhaps even inclined to divide them sharply into categories. In that case, she would fall into an untouchable category, for the snippets of publicity he had received usually paired him off with some beautiful, languid creature who had never done a day's work in her life. Anyway, Meg did not anticipate the kind of problem she sometimes had had to deal with at the restaurant.

She remembered a picture she had once seen of him, photographed against a background of mountains—a man of action, his hair ruffled by the wind. It had been a craggy, intelligent face, too, with dark eyes that looked directly into the camera and retained a smile in their depths. His mouth had been beautiful—a man's mouth—but with well-shaped, sensual lips that quirked slightly. One automatically knew that he was self-assured, even arrogant, a man who would have no trouble attracting any woman he wanted.

Meg blinked, caught by surprise as the lift doors slid noiselessly open. The doorbell was answered by a paunchy little man in a tightly belted raincoat. There was something familiar about him, although Meg was certain she had never met him. But apparently, he knew *her*.

'Come in, Miss Somers.' He held the door open.

She stepped hesitantly across the threshold.

'I was right, Mr Egan.' His eyes slid past her shoulder.

'Okay, Selby. If you're sure, you may go.'

It was a deep, lazy drawl, delivered in a dark-brown, velvet voice, and Meg felt a thrill of interest as she turned, smilingly. But there was no answering smile in the dark eyes that met hers. For a couple of instants, long enough that she knew she hadn't imagined it, there was a glimpse of ice there, a grim tautness in his face. He doesn't like me! But—why? Her mind raced. Was it her, or did he simply not like having to break in a new secretary?

Her smile faltered in the face of his chilly regard. 'Miss Somers.' He nodded distantly. 'You're early.'

His hostility unnerved her and she found herself rushing into a burst of nervous chatter. 'Y-yes, I—I'm sorry.' Could that be what was wrong? 'I—guess I was eager to meet you, Mr Egan.' She giggled uncertainly. 'It's not every day that one gets to meet a famous writer.'

His face was impassive. 'Are you impressed by famous writers, then?'

'Impressed?' Her lashes fluttered nervously. 'Perhaps—a little—but I am interested in learning everything I can from you.' She knew she was babbling and that it sounded silly but his coldness intimidated her.

'Indeed?' he drawled. 'This way, Miss Somers.'

She followed him into the living-room, which was a

luxuriously furnished but impersonal room, saved from total blandness by a magnificent view of the ocean from the balcony windows.

'Here. Sit down and let's talk.'

Meg sat down reluctantly, perching on the edge of the chair. Meantime, Simon Egan had stretched out with insolent ease in another chair, a can of beer balanced on his chest.

'Mrs Rogers assured me you were quite competent. Did she mention what I was doing here?'

'Researching for a new novel?'

'Yes. I intend to place my next book in Florida. Old Florida. There are some wonderful stories about its early history, but—you probably know that?' he added casually.

He was watching her keenly, and he couldn't miss the look of interest that sprang into her eyes. In spite of herself, Meg was intrigued. As a Floridian, she knew all the old stories about her state's past, its long years of Spanish rule, its background of pirates, smugglers, the slave trade . . . A historical novel was a departure from Egan's usual style, and Meg felt a tug of longing to be in on its conception.

'I need someone to transcribe my rough notes into something I can work with,' he was going on. 'As a general rule, I stay about two weeks ahead of my typist, and I have a stack of work over there.' He waved towards a desk littered with papers and a typewriter. 'Do you think you can keep up with me?'

She shifted uneasily. 'That part doesn't bother me,' she said slowly.

'Then what does?'

'I don't like the hours.' She stared at him stonily. 'I don't want to work at night.'

'Ah.' He smiled at her blandly. 'I have a solution to that.'

'Really?' Her voice iced.

'You could live here—with me. I have an extra bedroom and it would be convenient for me to have you—available—at all times.' To her indignant ears, he had bracketed the word with significance. 'Also,' he went on smoothly, 'you'd get to save on the rent, which will mean a rise in salary. That must be important for a girl like you.'

She stood up angrily. She was used to dealing with passes and she could deal with this one—in one of several ways. She could be gentle and not bruise the big lug's swollen ego, or she could use sledgehammer tactics. In this case, she didn't think anything less than sledgehammer tactics would satisfy her thirst for retribution.

'Mr Egan,' she began furiously, 'I think there has been some misunderstanding about what "type of girl" I am. I don't know if you got the wrong impression from Mrs Rogers, when she told you I needed a job, or if I inadvertently gave it to you myself, but in any case, you're wrong about how far I'll go to get this job—and keep it. I'm quite a bright girl, you know,' she added grimly, 'I have my own teeth, and a perfectly good pair of arms and legs. I've been supporting myself since I was seventeen, and I certainly don't need to prostitute myself to——'

The awful words were out before Meg could stop them, even as she saw by the look on his face that there had been some equally awful mistake. He wasn't offended. He wasn't even shocked. Instead, he was *laughing*!

'Do you also look under the bed every night before you go to sleep, Miss Somers?' he enquired gently.

She knew what he meant. He was implying that she imagined ghosts and ghoulies and rapists hiding behind every curtain and under every bed. In other words, she was a suppressed spinster who had imagined a proposition.

She opened her mouth once or twice, then burst out angrily, 'You suggested that I live with you——'

'That you occupy the extra bedroom,' he corrected her blandly. 'And save your rent. Was it such an insulting suggestion?' He chuckled at the look on her face. 'Come, come, Miss Somers. I'll rephrase my invitation, if you think I should. Will you work for me and not live with me? Er, sorry—not live in my house?' He grinned wickedly.

Meg had a sinking feeling. Deep within her bones, she knew she hadn't imagined his hostility, although it may have led her to jump to a number of conclusions. But she wasn't imagining he was enjoying her embarrassment! She flushed angrily, determined she wasn't going to apologise and she wasn't going to grovel.

'Are you sure you want me?' she asked levelly.

'I'm afraid to answer that on the grounds that it might incriminate me.' His eyes were gleaming with amusement. 'Don't look so stricken,' he surprised her by adding drily. 'You're an astute young lady and I owe you an apology. For everything. Will you accept it— and come to work for me?'

She stared at him sharply, meeting his bland gaze head-on. What he was admitting, in effect, was nothing and his blanket apology covered whatever she chose to interpret it should. But, she nodded slowly. 'If you like, Mr Egan.'

'Please—Simon. And may I call you Meg? I don't like formality.'

She agreed and he went on to discuss the terms of her employment. It was settled that she would come in the following morning. On the way down in the lift, Meg realised what a subtle man he was. He had disarmed her by apologising just as she was on the verge of leaving. Had he known that? Yes, she was sure he had. He had wanted her badly enough to humble himself which, in view of that odd flash of hostility in the beginning, didn't make sense. And what made even less sense was why? He had been prepared to dislike her almost from the start. According to Carol, she was a dull, open book, easily readable to anyone who cared to look. She had been tense and uneasy with Simon Egan, yet very impressed. Had he picked up that troubled awareness and was issuing some kind of warning? It made her squirm to think of it.

For a woman of Meg's age and time, a woman whose looks promised so much, Meg was really a novice when it came to men. She had never had time for the usual boy-girl relationships that led, inevitably, to sexual experience. She had always been too busy, working too hard. At the restaurant, she had heard a lot of talk that gave her a superficial knowledge, but she had never been tempted to experiment. She had been protected by Pierre, at first because of her age, then later, because he coldly decided he wanted her for himself. She had no way of judging a man like Simon Egan. She had no experience to guide her, merely an instinct that so far had kept her from making mistakes. And obviously, which had led her astray this afternoon, she acknowledged wryly.

She found a place to live that same afternoon, a motel room with a tiny kitchen, at a rent she could afford. It was old and shabby but it was only a few blocks from Simon's hotel, and close to a market and a chemist.

The rest of the day was spent in transferring her things, calling Helen, shopping for a few necessities and on impulse, stopping in at a bookstore and picking up a copy of Simon's latest novel, *Flashfire*, which she hadn't yet read.

Looking at his picture on the back cover all of her earlier reservations, plus a few more, crowded back. She didn't know if she even liked him. She certainly didn't trust him. But she wanted badly to work for him. It would be an experience she would never forget and if she made good, it would see her through a lean year while she learned to paint. It wouldn't be easy; instinctively, she knew he would expect perfection, or as near to it as was possible to achieve. He would drive her as hard as he did himself. But she had something to prove now.

Her first day at work set the pattern for the days that followed. Simon was asleep when she arrived, the work neatly stacked for her beside the typewriter. By noon, he awakened but she did not see him until he appeared, freshly showered, shaved and dressed, for coffee in the kitchen. Meg caught the fresh, pungent whiff of soap and shaving lotion as he passed behind her chair. Later, he reappeared with his coffee cup in hand, and grinned at her lazily.

'How about ringing downstairs to the restaurant and have them send up a breakfast? They know what I want—two eggs, bacon, toast, juice. And order whatever you want for lunch.'

'You must have worked late,' Meg commented primly as she pulled the 'phone towards her.

'I did. Until past four in the morning.'

When the cart was trundled upstairs, they broke off to eat, and began to talk. It was casual stuff at first, mostly on his part, with Meg asking tight little questions and ready to retreat at the first sign he was bored or irritated. He had been working on a television script for *Flashfire*, and he talked about that. He didn't like doing what he called a hatchet job on his novel, but he preferred to write the script himself than have someone else chop it to pieces. Meg, who had finished the book the night before, was curious to know how he was fitting a novel of that scope into a three-hour television play.

The next day, they lingered a little longer over their coffee. Meg had begun to type the script by that time and they discussed the changes he had made in converting the novel. Gradually, they spoke of other things, novels she had liked, he had liked, plays, movies, everything, in fact, but the blundering misunderstandings of that first meeting. He took the lead—he seemed genuinely to want to get to know her better.

A few nights later, Meg stayed on and cooked a Chinese dinner for him, because, he said, he was anxious to get some work out and needed her to type it. After that, sharing dinner, staying late, became a regular thing.

By the end of the second week, Meg was hooked on Simon Egan.

She didn't know she was hooked. It had been a subtle sort of wooing, happening so gradually she wasn't aware of it or anything except that she was experiencing the heady pleasure of meeting with another mind attuned perfectly to her own, one that stimulated her into thinking more deeply than she had in years.

For years, Meg had existed in a vacuum. Her life had been stunted at seventeen. College and the chance of a career had been permanently chopped off in the bud when she quit school and went to work for Pierre. Work was his god, and he made it hers, too. For mental stimulation, she had the conversation of the waitresses and busboys. At home, there was no one but Carol, whose conversation was almost always about herself and her own concerns.

Having been stifled in a nowhere job and a nowhere life for a long time now, suddenly, a new world had opened up. After a long, dry spell in a parched desert, it was heady stuff. So far, she wasn't aware of what was happening, but she was fast becoming addicted to Simon Egan, as surely as an addict develops a craving for a narcotic. For one who had always fiercely guarded her independence, she was allowing herself to drift into a dangerously dependent state. It never occurred to her that she might fall in love and lose her head over him or any man, although a few times she did think about how much she was going to miss him. He was a fascinating man, and a girl was going to have a problem if she started comparing every other man she met to him.

Then, the following week, Meg slammed into the truth with the speed of a runaway car.

Simon was up and taking a shower when she let herself into the apartment Monday morning with her key. That alone was a departure from the norm, and Meg fingered the papers at her typewriter, noticing that no work had been done since she had left Friday night.

Suddenly, the 'phone rang, startling her, and she picked it up cautiously. A warm, bubbly voice asked, 'Is Simon—Mr Egan there?'

Meg listened. 'He's in the shower right now.'

There wasn't a trace of astonishment in the other voice. Apparently, the woman, whoever she was, had been told all about her and her working arrangement. 'Oh, good!' The voice dropped to an intimate coo. 'I wasn't sure he'd got home yet. Tell him I left some of my make-up over there and he left his tie over here. We can do a swap when he comes tonight. Or—on second thoughts—don't worry him about it. I can pick up my make-up the next time I'm over there.'

Why don't you just do that? Meg thought sourly, as she dropped the 'phone. And why call? unless you want me to know you were with him over the weekend.

She pulled the typewriter towards her and was hard at work when Simon walked in. She noticed the hair at the nape of his neck was damp and curling slightly. Wet like that, it gleamed like ebony. There was a healthy glow about his skin as though he and Bubbly Voice had spent a lot of the weekend out of doors.

'You didn't get much work done this weekend, did you?' she asked.

'Uh, no, I didn't.' Following her usual custom, Meg had ordered his breakfast when she heard the shower, and he was attacking it hungrily. He looked sleepy, his lashes sweeping the lean, brown cheekbones. Heavy night! Meg thought caustically.

'You got a message,' she commented stiffly.

'Oh?' He didn't sound too interested.

'Something about picking up your tie tonight.'

'Okay.' He was reading a page she had typed and he began making corrections with a pencil.

'You must have had a busy weekend?'

He didn't look up. 'I did,' he agreed absent-mindedly.

'Have you known her long?'

He looked up at that, his eyes narrowing on her face. A brief grin slashed dimples in his cheek. 'Not long. Why?'

'Oh, I was curious. I didn't know you knew anyone in the city.'

'It's easy to meet a girl like Cindy. Now, about this page,' he sailed it across the table. 'I want to change the last paragraph. You'll see where I pencilled in the corrections.'

They worked in easy silence until noon, when Simon rose and stretched. 'I think I'll give my legs a break and walk down to the pizza place. Mushrooms and pepperoni all right with you?'

'Fine.'

It was the first time Meg had been alone in the apartment. She had been in every room except Simon's bedroom and she was consumed with curiosity. She told herself she was going to look for Cindy's make-up, but she knew that she wanted to see the room where Simon slept.

The maid hadn't been up to clean yet and his bed was still tumbled with sheets and blankets. He was apparently a restless sleeper. Meg looked at it wonderingly. Apparently, he had slept at home at least part of the night, in spite of Bubbly—no Cindy's—innuendo. His bed still held the faintly musky scent from his body. When she leaned over his pillow and smoothed her hand across it, she disturbed the clean shampoo fragrance he had left.

'What are you doing in here?'

Meg gasped and whirled.

Simon was standing in the doorway, legs planted apart, big, domineering and faintly menacing.

Meg whitened with shock and said the first thing that popped into her head.

'Why are you back so soon?'

He strolled into the room. 'I forgot my money.' The dark eyes were studying her face, but the menace had disappeared. He was even looking faintly speculative. 'I repeat—what are you doing in my room?'

'I—I——' She was totally unnerved and her mind refused to function. He continued to wait, watching her with unswerving eyes, until she finally gasped, 'C-Cindy said she left her make-up here. I—I was looking f-for it——'

His lip curled. 'In my bed?' he asked drily. 'An earring perhaps—but make-up? Definitely, no. Did you try the bathroom?'

Her flush deepened until she was on fire. 'I—No, I'll look there——' she gasped in a strangled whisper. She started to pass him but he gripped her arm and held her, ignoring the panicky attempts she was making to fight free.

'What were you *really* doing in here?' he asked grimly.

'I told you!'

'You told me nothing!' he snapped. 'Are you sure you weren't searching my room for money? You might expect to find my wallet under my pillow, for instance.'

'*What?*'

Her jaw dropped with astonishment. His eyes narrowed on her stunned face, seeing for himself that he had made the wrong assumption.

'If that's not it, what is it, then?' he asked roughly. 'Is

it possible you *were* searching for an earring?' He dragged her unwilling face around with hard hands to meet his. Eyeing her with dawning enlightenment, he went on slowly, 'You wanted to see if Cindy slept with me last night, didn't you? Blackmail, Miss Somers, or—jealousy?'

'Blackmail?' she repeated blankly. *'No!'*

'Then I'll have to conclude it was jealousy.' She saw a glint of amused mischief in the depths of his eyes and she squirmed with embarrassment. 'That's it, isn't it?' he taunted. His warm breath stirred the hairs at her temple. 'You're jealous—and if you're jealous—it follows you're interested in me.' He added deliberately, 'Is it possible I've got through to you, at last?'

'Please!' She struggled frantically to get away. 'I—I was wrong to come in here, but please, let me go!'

'No, you weren't wrong at all,' he drawled softly, pulling her into his arms. 'In fact, it may have been the first right thing you've done since you've been here. You've been a puzzle to me, Miss Somers, sitting so primly at your typewriter every day with your beautiful long legs tucked under the desk and your ripe, red lips a temptation. Ever since our first meeting, you've been putting out contradictory signals that have kept me confused as hell. After you chopped me off that first time, I decided I had it wrong, but now, I feel like a man who's finally picked up his trail again after losing it. I was right about you, after all, wasn't I?' Lowering his head, he ran a delicate tongue across her mouth, caressing its outlines until she trembled. His tongue was so soft on her silken flesh that it barely touched it, but wherever it touched, her skin reacted with a tingling flame. She moaned, fighting the compulsion to meet the challenge of that questing tongue, and he laughed softly. 'What's the matter, sweetheart?' he whispered. 'Don't you want to?'

Meg shuddered, filled with a sick self-contempt that

she had been so transparent. Oh, he knew women so well, and she must have been fairly obvious. But she wasn't a Cindy and she had no intention of being a pushover in a casual sexual encounter. She began to struggle in earnest.

But he pulled her sharply into his arms, letting her feel the hard, aroused muscles of his thighs. This time, he was hard and demanding, forcing an entrance to her mouth and then plundering its depths with a sensuality that made her weak with desire. His hands explored her body with a wanton frankness that sent the blood thundering through her veins. She had just enough sense to stand still and let him have his way, for she knew to fight him now would be to bring on what she was trying to avoid. He fumbled at her zip and the front closure of her bra, then for the first time in her life, Meg felt a man's hand on the soft weight of her breast, a man's mouth tugging at the soft bud in the centre. The resultant kick of pleasure was totally unexpected, and she drew in a long, sobbing breath that ended in a shudder. He looked at her. Her eyes were closed, the long lashes fanning her pale cheeks, the tears seeping from beneath the lids. Then, she felt his lips at the edge of her eyelids, licking the dampness from her lashes before trailing a line of small, nipping kisses across her face. He paused, his warm breath an erotic shiver across her heated skin.

'You're so beautiful,' he murmured. 'So very beautiful.'

His lips were weaving a shivering path across her face now—his roving hands creating a drowsy state of sensuality. When he kissed her, her lips clung to his with a warm, drugging sweetness. 'Put your arms around me,' he whispered. 'Touch me.' Hesitantly, her arms rose and clasped his neck, and she began to run her hands hungrily through his crisp black hair then trace, with a sense of wonderment, the harsh contours of his mouth and cheekbones. When her soft fingertips wandered into his mouth, he drew in his breath sharply, his eyes burning fiercely into hers.

Dimly, she realised that he was lifting her and that she should make some kind of protest, but she was delirious with pleasure. Her skin was hot and flushed, and the heated fumes had risen to her brain, clouding it to the knowledge that she was dangerously close to the point of no return.

He lowered her to the bed, his mouth clinging loosely to her swollen breast, and Meg's head fell back limply against the pillow. The clean scent of Simon's shampoo rose from the linen and penetrated her nostrils, mingling with the subtle fragrance of an expensive perfume. Meg's nose quivered and she froze with shock.

He was quick to pick up the change in her. Instantly, his hand gripped her chin and turned her head until he could see her face.

'What's the matter?' he asked quietly.

She stared directly into his eyes, making hers bitter and cool. 'Let me up, Simon. I made a mistake, that's all.'

He swore explicitly. 'You damn little tease! That I won't do.'

'I've changed my mind,' she cried desperately. 'You wouldn't force a woman, would you?'

His eyes narrowed and hardened. 'Not at all,' he drawled contemptuously. 'If I did, I might find myself facing a rape charge, mightn't I?'

Her face flamed. 'You have a right to be angry but not to throw an accusation like that in my face! It's just——' She swallowed. 'I—I can't make love on a bed that smells of another woman's perfume.'

He stared at her impassively. 'I want you,' he said in a hard, impersonal voice. 'What do I have to do to get you in my bed?'

'Not a damn thing!' she cried angrily. 'I don't sleep

around. The whole thing's been a mistake. I don't make casual love, in spite of what you might think.'

'Neither do I,' he said quickly. 'I'm past the age of enjoying one-night stands. You'll be my woman as long as I'm in Florida.'

'You aren't listening,' she said wearily. 'I don't have affairs.' She shivered and he stood up reluctantly.

'Are you talking about *marriage*?' he asked in a hard voice that held more than a hint of sarcasm.

She flinched. 'What's wrong with marriage?' she asked half defiantly. Her eyes dropped. 'I'm not proposing,' she muttered.

'And neither am I!' He gave a harsh laugh. 'My God, you do aim high, don't you?' He picked up her dress and tossed it to her. 'Get dressed and get back to work. You still have plenty to do. I'm going for that pizza, and I suggest you order your lunch as usual from downstairs.'

'Yes, boss,' she muttered under her breath, zipping herself hurriedly into her dress. She was past embarrassment, past even the humiliation of having gained his amused contempt. She was merely numb and wanted nothing more than to quietly fade into the background.

At her desk, he paused before leaving the apartment. 'I won't be back today,' he said quietly. 'When you've finished what you've got there, you're free to go.'

She nodded and kept typing. She had ruined everything by snooping through his room, then with her stupid, childish blowing hot and cold. She had acted like a frigid little tease. He had suspected her of thievery, blackmail, crying rape, and she couldn't blame him at all! She had been a fool. And then, to make that stupid, juvenile remark about marriage. Nowadays, girls didn't automatically assume that every man who wanted to take them to bed wanted marriage, too! Why, that philosophy belonged to Grandma's time. She had probably scared the man to death.

She sat on at the typewriter, unmoving, all thoughts of ordering her lunch forgotten. She was shocked at her own behaviour and thoroughly appalled at the glimpse she had got into Simon's mind. She wanted to crawl, not walk, to the nearest exit and then run a hundred miles, but at the same time, she knew she couldn't leave this job. She had to hang on as long as she could, because she couldn't give up seeing Simon. He had become necessary to her now, his good opinion of her as important as the breath she drew. She had to try to get herself back on the old footing.

CHAPTER THREE

THE following Sunday, it was windy and cool, a crisp hint of what winter would be like in this northern Florida city. Meg put on jeans and a bright red pullover, then struck out for the beach with her sketching pad. Her hair was soon a mass of tangles but it wasn't cold in the shelter of the dunes. Squatting on the sand, she opened her pad and soon became absorbed in sketching two sea gulls fighting over a candy wrapper. When she finished, she had got something of the look of cruelty in their eyes, with the wild, blowing day in the background.

'Hi! What are you doing?'

She looked up, startled. Simon was bending over her, wearing jogging shorts and a loose cable knit sweater. His eyes were on her sketch.

'That's good.' He crouched beside her. She was disturbed by the glimpse she had got of brown male flesh gleaming through the cable knit, and the fleeting brush of naked thighs against hers. It reminded her of the several mornings this week when she had arrived to find Simon in the kitchen, drinking coffee, wearing his bathrobe. It had been obvious every time that he wore nothing beneath the bathrobe. She stirred uneasily and tried to shift away.

'You're good,' he repeated, leafing through the pad. 'Why on earth are you working for me instead of putting your talent to work?'

'I have to eat,' she returned lightly.

'Don't give me that!' he said impatiently. 'You have talent. You can make a living with it. I don't like to hear you belittling it.'

She flushed. 'I wasn't doing that!' she protested. 'I intend to concentrate on my art someday, but right now, I need to earn some money to keep me while I go to art school.'

'Why waste your time and money on business school, then?'

'It's a long story,' she said crossly, knowing it would be impossible to explain her logic to Simon. It was all mixed up with not putting one's eggs all in one basket and the ingrained habits of economy taught to her by Mom, who always argued the wisdom of having another profession to fall back on if her art failed.

'In other words, the pickings are richer in the business world,' he returned cynically.

'That's not it at all!' Meg cried indignantly. 'I—It's hard to explain——'

But he wasn't listening. 'What's this?' he asked curiously. She looked over his shoulder. He was looking at some scenes she had sketched from the book he was writing. It was to be a historical drama—a complete departure from his usual hard-hitting modern adventure yarn—and she had sketched scenes of old Florida. There was one of a sailing ship, a timbered fort, a hanging tree with a kangaroo court of pirates beneath it, and the complete isolation of a beach, complete with scrub palms and sand dunes.

'I was thinking about your book the other night——' she began embarrassedly.

'They're exactly what I had in mind.' He stared at her thoughtfully, then held out his hand. 'Let's see what you can do when you don't have to use your imagination. There's an old bridge near here I'd like to have sketched.'

She got up quickly and began to brush the sand off her jeans, thrilled at the opportunity to be meeting Simon on what was more or less neutral ground, and hopefully, re-establishing their old comradeship.

Things had been rather sticky this week and looking back, Meg knew it had been her fault, not his. He had not fired her—to her relief—and he seemed to have successfully put the whole episode behind him. In fact, he treated her with casual uninterest. But Meg had been unable to meet him halfway. She had been stiff and self-conscious. She could not look at Simon without remembering those impassioned kisses they had shared, the fact that he had caressed her near-naked body. She could not talk to him as a casual friend when they had almost been lovers. And although the episode apparently meant nothing to Simon, it had been of tremendous importance to her. She did not know if she was in love with Simon—she hoped not, for she knew it could come to nothing—but she was aware of him with every fibre of her being. She desperately wanted to regain the old footing and accept his friendship—and this was a beginning.

In fact, it felt very satisfying to be rambling through the countryside, sketching, and later assembling the makings of a picnic from the contents of a little country store near the beach. And later, when they drove into the parking lot of the shabby little carport, Simon's friendliness gave her the courage to say shyly, 'Would you care to have dinner with me tonight? It's only spaghetti,' she stumbled on, 'but I have enough. You wouldn't be putting me out.'

The dark eyes surveyed her thoughtfully, then he smiled. 'Sure. Why not?'

It was an event and Meg was anxious to have everything right. As he prowled about the room, she boiled the pasta and heated the sauce which she had made the day before and refrigerated.

She was thankful that she had tidied up before leaving that morning. Nothing would make the room anything but a shabby beach rental but she had made it attractive by pushing the bed against the wall and adding cheap colourful cushions to give it the appearance of a couch. She had added more cushions and her mother's afghan to the worn plastic armchairs, and on the dresser, her photographs shared a place with a jam jar of yellow chrysanthemums.

Simon picked up the double photograph of her parents and asked about them. She found herself talking freely as she made salad and garlic bread. She told him about her mother's death, her father's second marriage and the closeness she had shared with Mom before her death.

'This must be your stepmother, then?'

He had picked up the picture of Alice and Carol, taken when Carol was about eleven.

She looked up from tossing the salad. 'Yes, that's Mom.'

'And the little girl is your stepsister?'

'Yes,' she said briefly.

'Older or younger than you?'

'Younger. Carol is eighteen.'

'Where is she now?'

'Miami.'

'With relatives?'

'No,' she said shortly. 'There were no relatives.'

He must have sensed her reluctance but he persisted. 'She was a beautiful child. Is she still this lovely?'

'Yes.'

'What's she doing? In college? Working? Married?'

'I don't know what she's doing.'

'What does that mean?' He stared at her. 'Haven't you kept up with her? She's only eighteen, not much more than a child, and unless——'

'No, I haven't kept up with her! The last time I saw her, she was going off to live with a man! Satisfied?' She exploded with bitter passion, banging the plates on the table. 'Look! Carol is perfectly able to take care of herself! I assure you, she doesn't need me! And isn't this my business anyway?'

'You're right. It *is* your business. Sorry,' he added indifferently, picking up his fork.

Meg realised she had somehow put herself in the wrong and she attempted to make a halting explanation. 'It's not that I don't—didn't—care,' she began awkwardly. 'It's just that Carol——'

He interrupted. 'You don't owe me any explanation. We've both agreed it's none of my business so let's drop the subject, shall we? It's begun to bore me.'

Under the circumstances, she had no course but to do as he said. It was too late to correct it now but she hoped she'd have a chance soon to explain about Carol. She knew that she had left a bad impression through her own shrinking reluctance to discuss the circumstances of her parting. She knew, too, that it was important that Simon think well of her, and she regretted that Carol—of all people!—had come between them.

As he was leaving, he stooped to give her a chaste good night kiss and Meg responded fiercely, pride forgotten as her lips clung hungrily to his. He drew back sharply, frowning as he searched her face. For a moment, before she could control her expression, it was all there in her face for him to see—the mingled feelings of longing, desire, pleading... His eyes gleamed with a sudden understanding before he veiled them with heavy lids.

'I'm going to St Augustine this weekend,' he said deliberately. 'Would you like to go with me?'

Meg knew she had given herself away. She knew what he was asking her and what it would mean if she agreed to go. They would be sharing a bed.

'I'd like your impressions of the old fort,' he added drily when she said nothing. 'Naturally, I'll pay you for your time. And your expenses.'

She flushed. 'I would enjoy sketching the old fort and I won't charge you a cent!' she said crisply, before she realised from his expression that she had, in effect, agreed to go.

It was too late then to change her mind even if Meg had wanted to. After he was gone, she faced up to the reality that her heart had been trying to tell her all week: she was in love with Simon. It was already too late to back away—her love, once given, could not be taken back. Simon did not love her. She accepted that it would mean the eventual ending of the affair between them. She could already anticipate the pain. But she knew this might be her last chance to love him and if she didn't seize it, she would regret it forever. She had been right to agree to go.

'Have you ever been to St Augustine?' he asked as they drove south along the coastal highway, the next day.

'No, never.' She smiled at him, her eyes very green in the mellow sunlight. She and Simon were back on the old footing and all her doubts and uncertainties about what this trip would mean had vanished, like a puff of smoke on the wind. Simon had made it clear in so many little ways, ever since she had agreed to come, that he wanted her. She would sleep with her love tonight and tomorrow, she would wake beside him. And that was all that mattered.

They were taking in all the tourist traps along the road, and that included the inevitable ticky-tacky souvenir stands. They made a bet to see who could find the most vulgar souvenir. Meg's choice was a plastic alligator with a clock in his navel, but when Simon came up with a model of an outdoor privy with an alligator perched inside, Meg had to admit he had won. She paid off with lunch next door to the souvenir stand. Simon ordered a foot-long hot dog with all the trimmings. The trimmings included fifteen items that could be eaten with a hot dog and Simon chose twelve, then couldn't get his mouth around it. The results were hilarious with Meg mopping him up with paper napkins.

By the time they reached the hotel, they were as grubby as children, their arms and faces sun-kissed. She followed Simon into the hotel. At the desk, Simon asked for two rooms and took what they gave him, which happened to be adjoining rooms. They rode up in the lift together and he tipped the bellboy who carried in Meg's bag, then stood casually in the doorway while they made plans for dinner. Then he left her.

Meg felt rather blank. She didn't know what she had expected but not this. She told herself it was unrealistic to assume they would share a bedroom after she had made her views clear on that subject to Simon. Obviously, Simon intended to wait until later, after dinner, and in that regard, Meg had provided herself with a formidable arsenal. It had looked like nothing in the dress shop—a little black dress that the salesgirl had talked her into trying on. But with rhinestone loops in her ears, and her hair loose on her shoulders, it provided a stunning contrast to her white skin and flame-coloured hair. Her cleavage dipped low, providing an enticing glimpse of her breasts, and the rippling skirt showed off her long, slim legs. Meg had experimented with eye make-up that deepened and accentuated her green eyes and a bright lustrous lipstick that matched her nail enamel. The dress was provided with a little jacket that kept it within discreet bounds, but Meg descended with it over her arm. She intended for Simon to get the first impact or the dress before she added the jacket.

As she left the lift, she looked around for Simon and saw him at the desk, talking to the manager. He was wearing a supple leather coat and a shirt of heather mix, and she noticed wryly that he was getting a fair amount of attention from the women in the lobby. Meg was unaware that she herself was drawing her share of male looks.

It was her first time to see him in relation to other people and she realised how strong an aura he carried with him—an aura of power and success. His features were too harshly defined to be considered handsome, but he had that superb arrogance that conveys a natural authority and passes for good looks. In a crowd, he would draw all eyes and most of the feminine ones twice. It brought home to her as nothing else could just how presumptuous she was to dream of a future with a man like this. It was an unsettling thought and Meg moved forward swiftly, her high heels a muted tap on the marble floor. He turned at once, sensing her presence before he saw her.

Her lips parted breathlessly. 'I'm sorry I kept you waiting.'

'It was worth it.' He surveyed her impersonally. 'You look very lovely. This is the real you, I suspect, not that scruffy urchin in jeans.'

'That scruffy urchin had her place.' She smiled slowly. 'But every girl likes to dress up in beautiful clothes and wear expensive perfume occasionally.'

'Some more than others, no doubt,' he agreed cynically. 'And why not? If she can look like you.'

His cynicism was disturbing but Meg tried to ignore it. After that, however, the tone had been set for the evening—light, flirtatious and wholly casual. Meg knew before the end of it that Simon had no intention of making love to her tonight. She was puzzled and disconcerted. Had she misread the entire situation?

They dined at a seafood place that could be reached by walking from their hotel. From the window, they could see the lights of the old fort, the Castillo de San Marcos, which dominated the landscape of St Augustine. Afterwards, instead of going to the lounge of the hotel that featured a band and dancing, Simon headed for the cocktail bar and its piano player. They had a liqueur and then, he suggested they make an early night of it. She left him at the table, finishing his second brandy and making casual conversation with the bartender.

The next day, Meg was frankly on edge. They toured the fort, where she made some sketches from the battlements. Then, they strolled through the state run village of San Augustin Antiquo, the historical restoration area. There, just beyond the coquino pillars of the old city gate, was St George Street, the first street in the oldest city of the New World. Totally Spanish in character, it was cobblestoned and bright with flowers from the balconies that jutted out overhead. Meg tried to see it as it must have been then, when a strange frightening continent lay just beyond the fringe of the forests.

That night, they dined at an inn that had been highly recommended in the guide books. It lived up to its expectations, with a menu that Pierre's La Frontand would have trouble surpassing. A first course of Oysters Rockefeller with crabmeat was followed by Chateaubriand, accompanied by baby potatoes and carrots. Instead of dessert, Simon chose a slice of Brie with grapes and apple slices, but Meg succumbed to the lure of Amaretto soufflé. He watched her indulgently as she licked the last delectable morsel clinging to her lip, and then suggested that they have liqueurs with their coffee. Meg chose Grand Marnier.

By this time, she was feeling slightly tipsy and when they got outside, the cool air, hitting her flushed cheeks, made her stumble.

'Oops,' she giggled, clutching Simon's arm.

He laughed as he assisted her into the car, then went around to the other side to let himself in. 'I'm afraid that last drink was a mistake. But you're perfectly safe with me,' he added sardonically, and for emphasis, he leaned over and kissed her lightly on the lips.

'That's what I'm afraid of,' Meg murmured huskily, then remorsefully, 'I can't believe I said that.'

He chuckled. 'Remind me to take you up on that when we get back to the hotel.'

Meg waited with a growing mixture of alarm and anticipation until they were alone in the lift when he took her into his arms and kissed her deeply and sensuously. With growing passion, his lips explored her face before returning to her mouth. By this time, Meg's head was swimming as she clung to him, hungrily returning his kisses, letting him feel her eagerness and her warmth.

When the lift stopped, she was trembling so that she could hardly walk. He guided her to her door where he stopped and kissed her again. This time, he caressed her body until his touch on her sensitised skin was a torment.

'Sweet,' he murmured huskily. 'So sweet.'

Kissing the moan off her lips, he pushed her unresistingly towards the open door and she realised that at some time during the kiss, he had unlocked it. She went willingly, assuming he was following, but as soon as she was inside, he disengaged himself deftly from her clinging arms.

'You're going to have a headache in the morning,' he whispered mockingly, patting her cheek with a teasing forefinger. 'If you need me—or an aspirin—during the night, you know where to find me.'

And he closed the door in her disbelieving face.

She stared at it dumbly. Her body felt heavy and drugged with desire; her wits were definitely not at their best; but over and above all else, she was sickened with disappointment. She heard a low, mewing cry of pain and realised it came from her own throat. She started towards the door, intent on following Simon, and was stopped by the flashing movement of her own reflection in the mirror mounted on the bathroom door.

It reflected the body and face of a stranger. Meg stared at herself witlessly. Her face was flushed; her heavy-lidded eyes slumborous with passion; her mouth reddened and swollen. Her tousled hair strayed in witch locks across a naked breast. Stunned, her eyes travelled down to find that her dress had been pushed aside, exposing a ripe, throbbing breast crested by a hardened nipple. Abruptly, she was ice cold sober, her brain cleared of the drugging fumes of alcohol and unrequited passion.

Had she really been about to go to Simon's room? Looking like a stranger—a *harlot*! She remembered the way she had looked in this same mirror three hours earlier and she shuddered. Had she really sunk so low she would *beg* a man to make love to her? Her mouth twisted with the sour taste of self-contempt. In the heat of passion, perhaps; but after he had left her? Was this how she wanted to learn about love for the first time, half-drunk, totally abandoned, asking to be humiliated? *No!* She closed her eyes. Thank you, God, for saving me from destroying my self-respect. Simon had to know she wanted him—he wasn't dense—yet he hadn't stayed to make love to her. She didn't know why he had decided to let her do the running, but she couldn't do it. If she had gone to him, would he have spurned her? Perhaps not, but she knew in her bones he would have taken her without respect. And God knows, although she didn't have much pride left, she was too proud to allow herself to be used that way.

She gathered the tattered rags of her self-respect about her and went to the bathroom. Perhaps she should consider a cold shower, she thought wryly. For punitive reasons, if no other. And perhaps, at the same time, give another prayer of thankfulness that she had been given a second chance.

The next morning, she was standing in line at the breakfast buffet when he joined her. He looked tired and jaded and Meg wondered if he had waited for her last night until late. In that case, why had he left her? Unless it was a matter of petty revenge, and Meg couldn't believe Simon would be so small as to exact revenge for that other episode when she had spurned him. But it was a disquieting thought and as the waitress poured their coffee, Meg found herself studying the lines of strain in his face.

'By the way,' he remarked laconically. 'I'm returning to Jacksonville right after breakfast. I'm catching the afternoon plane for Denver.'

Shock held her silent. She was appalled by the overwhelming feeling of desolation. Was this goodbye? Had her pride driven him into making this decision?

She cleared her throat. 'Why Denver?' she asked huskily.

'That's my home, silly girl.' He sounded amused, the thick lashes raising to betray eyes of unexpected keenness as they centred on her white face.

'Are you coming back?' she whispered.

She had put down her spoon and wasn't eating but he was finishing his grapefruit with relish, as though he was suddenly enjoying his breakfast.

'I don't know,' he said bluntly. 'It depends.'

'On what?'

'Many things. Do you want me to come back?' he added softly, watching as the blood rose in her distressed face.

Pride went by the wayside. She swallowed painfully. 'Yes. Please do.'

'I might—if I thought you cared.'

Oh, God! She closed her eyes agonisedly. 'What can I do to prove I care?'

He grinned. 'I'll think of something.'

He would, too, the bastard! She flushed angrily. 'Not that!' she gritted.

He laughed softly, and leaning forward, stroked her

cheek. 'I'll be back,' he said carelessly. 'I have some things to do in Colorado, then I'll be back. You have a little holiday while I'm gone and wait for me.'

That was how he said goodbye, for he didn't want her to go with him to the airport. The Porsche was rented, and he had to turn it in. He left her the key to his hotel apartment, and her salary cheque for the next month. She took this as a good omen, an indication that he meant what he said. He would be coming back, and she clung to that thought in the month that followed.

Since there was no work for her to do, Meg forced herself to fill her days with activity. She began art classes and went to the movies a couple of times with school friends. She sketched, mostly portraits of Simon, whom she drew in a hundred different moods. She met Helen for dinner, and every day, she waited for some indication he would return. She had no idea how to get in touch with him. In her agitation that last day, she had forgotten to get his address!

Meg began to lose hope as November drew to a close. It would soon be Thanksgiving and then Christmas, and somehow, she couldn't see Simon returning to Florida for Christmas. The weather report said it was snowing in Colorado, and he had once said he liked to ski. She visualised him on the ski slopes of Aspen with a blonde. She would be someone he met at a ski lodge, someone he would make love to for that weekend, and when they parted, it would be with no regrets on either side, just the way he liked it.

Of course, he had no reason to want to see Meg again. He was a man who travelled light, without encumbrances, and he had recognised her instinctively as an encumbrance. An old-fashioned girl, the kind who wouldn't take their parting lightly—the kind who would have regrets. That was the reason he had shied off that last weekend. It was less embarrassing that way. And being a kind-hearted man, he would be uncomfortable if he was embarrassed. No, Meg faced the inevitable with quiet desperation. He wasn't coming back.

She was letting herself into her room after having dinner with Helen when her 'phone rang. It kept ringing as she struggled with the key, then frantically raced across the room in the dark, barking her shins on a chair on the way.

'Hello?' she asked breathlessly.

'Where were you?'

She sat down abruptly on the side of the bed and closed her eyes. Thank you, God, she breathed.

'What's the matter, darling? Aren't you talking to me?'

He often called her darling. That didn't mean a thing.

'When are you coming back?'

'Do you want me to come?'

'You know I do,' she returned lightly. 'I'm getting bored having nothing to do.'

'Good! Because I'm here.'

She drew in a sharp breath. 'Here!' Her voice rose. 'Here in Jacksonville? When? Are you here to stay?'

He laughed. 'Not so fast! I'll tell you all about it in the morning. Where were you, anyway? It's after ten!'

'I was having dinner with Helen. Mrs Rogers.'

'That's allowable,' he said gravely. 'See you in the morning,' and rang off.

The next morning, he hugged her when she walked in but did not kiss her. His tan had faded a little but he had been skiing, he said. But not at Aspen.

'Why Aspen?' He was amused. 'There are other places, you know. Would you like to visit Aspen?'

'Oh, no!' she disclaimed, anxious not to appear anxious.

'Too bad,' he said oddly, then went on to tell her he was leaving Florida. He had come back only to make arrangements about his things. In a couple of days, no more, he would be returning to Colorado, where he planned to spend the winter writing his novel.

Meg listened to him numbly, her hands tightly clasped in her lap, and nothing in her face gave any indication that her heart was being squeezed in a vice of pain and longing. He is leaving. Over and over the words beat their remorseless refrain in her brain until she thought she would faint. He is leaving and I am dying. And then, like a light at the end of a tunnel, the solution came to her. I am going with him. No longer was she going to allow herself the luxury of false pride. If it took begging, pleading, guile—she was going with him. She would promise no scenes when it was over. Absolutely not. When he got ready to depart for places unknown, she would wave him off with a smile. And he already knew he worked well with her. He would need a secretary, wouldn't he? If she kept her head and avoided emotionalism, he just might ... there was a good chance he might ...

'You don't need a good secretary, do you?' she asked brightly, playing it for laughs. She even smiled carelessly.

'No.' His negative was uncompromising.

She drew a deep, steady breath. 'I see.' Swallowing hard, she went on, 'Then, what about a cook? A mistress? Guaranteed to please, to stay out of your way until needed and to leave quietly when she's fired?'

He looked at her curiously. 'Are you offering for the position?'

'Yes.' Her heart was in her eyes.

'You didn't feel that way that night in St Augustine.' He smiled slightly. 'I waited, you know, for you to knock and ask to borrow an aspirin.' His smile was tinged with self-mockery. 'But you stayed sedately in your room. Why have you changed your mind now?'

'Oh, I don't know,' she said carelessly. 'I guess I fell in love with you.' She didn't try to tell him she'd been in love all along. 'Absence making the heart fonder and all that stuff.'

'I know all about it,' he said grimly. He sounded almost angry with himself. 'I fell in love, too.'

She stared at him round-eyed, uncomprehending. 'Wha-at?'

He grinned suddenly, his eyes lit with mischief, and Meg felt the tug of that charm he used quite ruthlessly when it suited him. 'Silly girl. Don't you recognise a proposal when you hear one?'

She started crying, the big tears rolling down her pale cheeks. 'Are you asking me to marry you?'

'Don't look so surprised,' he said gently, leaning forward and placing a warm kiss on her lips. Hers clung but he drew away. 'Surely you knew I was falling in love with you?'

She burst into tears and threw her arms around his neck, sobbing, 'No! No, I didn't! I really didn't! Are you sure? I mean—I'm not dreaming, am I?'

He pulled her face out of his shoulder and kissed it lightly. 'My dear Meg, don't be obtuse. Surely you suspected something was going on when I abandoned all attempts to get you in my bed and left the state? I had to get away in order to gain a perspective on my feelings, to be sure that what I felt was love. And if it justified asking you to become my wife. I'm not easy to live with, you know,' he added warningly.

But she was smiling. She was giddy with joy and in no mood to listen to anything but the singing happiness in her own heart. 'I'm not worried,' she said joyously, leaning her head against his neck.

'Not even when I bury myself in my work and don't surface for days on end?' he asked teasingly.

'No.'

'And you don't mind doing your own housework and

cooking? I loathe having servants cluttering up the place, you know.'

She drew back and gazed into his eyes. 'Is that the worst you can come up with, Mr Egan?' she asked saucily.

'No,' He smiled oddly. 'Give me time and I'll come up with something worse than that.'

'Well, meantime, you'll excuse me if I go ahead and marry you, please?'

'But, Miss Somers, ma'am, you haven't said "yes", yet!' he remonstrated. 'I'd like a proper answer to my proposal, if you please.'

'Yes, yes, *yes*!' She punctuated each word with a kiss. 'A thousand times! Oh, I'm going to love Colorado! I already do!'

If Simon was amazed at the change in Meg, he had a right to be. Before his eyes, she was turning into a new person, teasing, provocative, scintillating with happiness. He watched her with a smile as she rhapsodised about the future. Finally, she settled down to listen rationally as he explained why he wanted to leave at once for Denver. He wanted them to spend their honeymoon at his grandparents' lodge on a mountain top, and they must get there before the snows came. He would teach her to ski there, he said. Although he owned a home in Denver, he felt that a snowy mountaintop would be more appropriate for a honeymoon. Meg listened dazedly, too much in love to question anything he said.

'Umm,' she murmured, visualising the moonlight glinting on a snowbound cabin in the wilderness. 'I hope it snows and snows and snows, and we *never* have to come down off that mountain.'

'Do you?' He smiled slowly. 'Perhaps you'll get your wish. If it does, I'm prepared. That's what I've been doing these past weeks, once I made up my mind that I was going to ask you to marry me. I've been getting the old place ready for us by putting in a freezer, washer and drier, and getting the furnace in order.'

'What if I had said "no"?' Meg teased.

'Then I'd have spent the winter up there, typing and licking my wounds in private,' he replied drily. 'But you aren't, are you?'

'Not likely!' she said emphatically. 'Funny, I've been visualising you on the ski slopes of Aspen with a girl.'

He laughed. 'You and your Aspen. The only girl I want is right here. I wouldn't give up my status as a bachelor for just *any* girl, you know.'

She sobered. 'You don't have to marry me, you know.' She lifted shy eyes to his, trying to be painfully honest. 'You know, don't you, that you could have had me anytime without marriage? I was fairly obvious about it—you must have known. I'm not ashamed—I couldn't help it.'

He was regarding her with an odd smile. 'None of us can when the blood is hot,' he said gently. 'No, my dear, I want to marry you. Make no mistake about that. Nothing less will do, I've made my plans——'

'Plans can be unmade,' she said seriously.

'Are you trying to back out now?' he scolded her gently. 'When I've already applied for the licence? And brought in food and supplies? And . . .'

'All right, all right!' she bubbled. 'But, Simon, I haven't any clothes suitable for Colorado! Will I have time to buy some here before we leave?'

'Buy clothes in Florida that will do for Colorado? No way! We'll have to wait until we get there. Now, can you be ready to leave by tomorrow?'

She didn't hesitate. 'Of course.'

'Then, I'll let your last act as my secretary be to make our plane reservations. After that, you may go home and get ready to leave in the morning as early as possible. With any luck, we'll be married and on our mountaintop by the end of the week.'

CHAPTER FOUR

MEG bought her wedding clothes in Florida. She found just what she wanted in her favourite little shop, and although it cost a small fortune, it was worth it—gossamer lingerie and a wedding dress of white wool. Her accessories—a clutch-bag and delicate high-heeled pumps were of white suede. For her something blue, she intended carrying a fragile handkerchief that had belonged to her mother in her small clasp-bag.

After that, there was Helen to call and her art teacher, who recommended a good teacher in Denver, at the same time insisting that she continue her studies. That night, she had dinner with Simon at a French restaurant that was so much like Frontand's that Meg felt it put the final adieu to her old life. Then, after giving her a warm kiss that left her aching and unsatisfied, Simon left her at the door and told her to be ready the next morning.

He presented her with a ring after they were airborne, a big diamond that Carol would have envied. The luxurious first-class seats were almost as private as their own living-room but Simon would only permit chaste kisses to be exchanged. However, Meg found wearing the ring very satisfying. It set his seal of ownership on her and at the same time, proclaimed to the world that he was her man.

They were married in Denver four days later and left at once for Brennan's Pass, the little town near the mountain where they were to honeymoon. Meg was relieved to have the wedding over, for the four days were a strain. For one thing, she stayed at the hotel and Simon at home, but she was not even given an opportunity to view her future home. She hadn't liked to ask, since he didn't offer to show it to her. She hadn't wanted to act like a man-hungry female, either, but his kisses left her longing for more. It had been Simon's decision not to anticipate the wedding vows and although Meg concurred in principle, it was very hard to put into practice. It was much harder on Simon, of course she knew that, but he got over the difficulty by making his kisses more like friendly salutes than kisses between lovers.

In other ways, Simon was perfect. He was very generous, for one thing, allowing her to choose her wedding ring, and spending a stunning amount of money on the right kind of winter clothes for her. She had never seen clothes like that before—thick, wool ski pants; ski masks; fleece-lined boots and jackets; heavy, wool socks and wool mittens to go over gloves. She had never owned a pair of gloves in her life, much less mittens, and she had never *seen* a fleece-lined coat. In fact, she had never owned a winter coat, either, finding it a useless article of clothing in south Florida. So, she took Simon's advice on what to buy, although she teased him that he was preparing her for a siege.

She bought other things with her own money, things she thought of as trousseau clothes. Beautiful warm nightgowns and robes, as well as a couple of velvet caftans for evening. She was willing to accept that a snowstorm might occur during their honeymoon but she wanted to look glamorous while she was sitting it out.

The night before the wedding, she wandered restlessly through the little arcade of shops in the lobby of the hotel. In one, she saw a crystal paperweight with a burst of colourful geometric-shaped prisms in the centre, and she bought it for Simon as a wedding gift. It took most of the remainder of her money, but she liked it and wanted him to have something that would remind him of her while he was working.

It was well below freezing the next morning. The slush that was piled at the edge of the street was rimed with ice, and crunched beneath the wheels of the cars. The forecast predicted a cold front moving down from the north, bringing heavy snows. When Simon picked her up at the hotel, he was wearing heavy boots, a flannel shirt, a fleece-lined jacket, and looked more like a lumberjack than a bridegroom. He looked irritably at her wedding dress and shoes.

'Why didn't you choose something more suitable? Now, you're going to have to come back to the hotel and change! You can't travel in *that*!'

She was shaken by his abruptness. It was their wedding day—didn't he understand how she felt? Her already lowered morale wasn't improved later by the judge, nor the lack of flowers and friends, nor even a smile from the bridegroom. He thrust the wedding ring on her finger with a grim look of distaste for the whole affair and growled his responses. As they were signing the register, he said abruptly, 'By the way, Meg, I forgot to mention it, but your real name is now Melton, not Egan. Egan was my mother's name and I use it for my books, but my legal name is Melton.'

Meg straightened slowly and stared at him, shocked. 'But—why didn't you tell me?'

'Does it matter?' His voice was indifferent.

'Of *course* it matters!' she cried explosively.

'Why?'

She merely shook her head, unable to put into words her uneasiness, the suspicion that he had deliberately withheld the name change from her, but most of all, the avid way he had watched her face as he said his name. She frowned slightly, trying to put the whole thing out of her mind. Her new husband was definitely springing surprising new sides to his personality on her.

Back at the hotel, things didn't improve as he pawed through her packed cases and dug out an assortment of thick, heavy clothing. 'You'll need to dress warmly if you aren't to freeze,' he said impersonally, barely glancing at her half naked, shivering body. 'I'll take your luggage down and wait for you in the lobby.'

Meg tried to hurry, but in her nervousness, her fingers were all thumbs. She needed Simon here, reassuring her as he helped her into her clothes, perhaps kissing her occassionally. He hadn't kissed her since the peck he gave her at the wedding ceremony, and that didn't count. Of course, he was in a hurry to get started—he had already warned her that if the snow clouds to the north dumped their load prematurely, they wouldn't get up the mountain. The more she thought of it, the more she thought it might be a good idea to wait a while and get to know one another before spending a few weeks alone. Already, she was getting a sick headache worrying about things like the stranger waiting for her downstairs, and—tonight—and oh, other more practical things, such as heat, food and electricity. Simon had assured her that the power lines were safe because they went underground, and he could cope with any emergency that might arise, but with thoughts of hurricane disasters in her mind, Meg hadn't been altogether reassured.

She stamped her feet into her heavy boots and made her way to the lobby to find him waiting for her. If he was having second thoughts about where they were going, it didn't show as he hurried her into the waiting Jeep. He had told her it took a car like that to get up the mountainside, but it was an uncomfortable car to ride in and inclined to be draughty in places.

Meg had seen the mountains of North Carolina and Tennessee when she was a small girl, but these jagged black peaks, capped with snow, were a new breed. They frightened her. Sitting beside Simon, listening to the tyres sing as they bit the snowy road underfoot, Meg longed for comfort. She wanted him to turn and speak to her, but he was humming under his breath, his eyes fixed on the distant mountains in a far-seeing stare. She saw that he loved them, his mood was anticipatory. He couldn't possibly understand how she felt.

Things brightened a little when they stopped for hamburgers at lunchtime. Simon reminded her of the time they had had hot dogs together, and the teasing light in his eyes gave her the reassurance she had been seeking. After that, it was easy to fall asleep on Simon's shoulder while listening dreamily to the radio.

When she woke, the sun, which had been feebly trying to shine earlier, had disappeared and the landscape looked bleak and cold. A sign flashed by that read, 'Brennan's Pass, Population 247', and Meg knew they were almost at their destination. She blinked and sat upright, listening to a voice on the radio warning travellers of hazardous driving conditions. Snow had been falling steadily north of here, and travellers who planned to go straight through were warned to seek shelter for the night.

'Which we certainly intend to do,' Simon murmured comfortingly, glancing at her perturbed face. 'Had a good sleep?'

'Uh, huh.' She yawned and stretched. 'But I feel guilty, leaving you to do all the driving.' She felt safe in making the remark, knowing that Simon wouldn't have allowed her to drive anyway. She was ashamed for him to know that she hadn't driven since Mom's death, and handling a car in these conditions would have literally made her sick with fear. 'Are we nearly there?'

'It won't be long. That's our mountain over there.' He nodded towards a northern mountain range.

She was silent. But her doubts began to increase when, after stopping at a general store Simon got out and returned, carrying a box of supplies and followed by the grocer carrying another box. 'Where are you folks headed?' the man asked, stowing the boxes on the back floor of the Jeep.

Simon crawled in behind the wheel and turned the key. 'The old Egan place,' he said briefly.

The motor roared and the man stepped back hastily, but not before Meg glimpsed a look of surprise on his face. Before he could speak, the Jeep took off, spitting ice.

'That man seemed surprised,' she ventured.

'That's probably because he thinks we're a couple of fools,' Simon drawled sardonically.

'Fools?'

'Uh, huh. My grandfather's place has been closed for years.'

'Years?' she echoed faintly.

He looked coldly amused. 'I hope you aren't afraid of hard work.'

She stared at him confusedly. Where had she got the impression that the place was in constant use during the skiing season? She knew Simon hadn't said it had been closed up! And what exactly did that mean? What if they found it damp, unaired, dirty? And what about *heat*? Was Simon crazy?

When she timidly asked about heat, he reassured her. 'The furnace is okay. A little old, but I saw to it when I was up here last month. And I bought a freezer and filled it.' He saw her glance at the boxes. 'That stuff is food that won't freeze. Milk, eggs, lettuce, that sort of thing. When that goes, we'll have to go on dried and frozen food.'

She stared at him in consternation. 'But—how long are we going to stay?'

'Oh, we're spending the winter up there. Cosy, eh?' he added with a crooked smile.

'I . . . g-guess so,' Meg faltered blankly.

'I wonder if you'll be saying the same thing this time next month?' he asked blandly.

Meg smiled nervously, as uneasy as much by his attitude as the news that she had suddenly been given. Simon signalled for a left-hand turn, and they turned on to a mountain road. The snow ploughs had been at work, and the steady climb was gentle, the curves wide and well-angled. There was nothing frightening about the clear fields of unbroken snow on either side of the road.

Then Simon slowed and put the Jeep into whining first gear and Meg saw they were turning into a rutted track leading off the road. She gasped with horror as the Jeep slithered on the frozen ice, before its tyres bit and held. The motor changed tempo and the curves grew sharper as the shoulder fell off to a sheer drop below. At one point, she allowed herself a stricken glance downward and saw the wide, snowswept road far below them, angling off between the mountains. *They* were going straight up the mountain on a road that seemed to her, at least, dangerously narrow and soon to be impassable. At this point, however, there was no place to go but up, for the Jeep certainly couldn't turn around. It was climbing already at a crawl, its labouring motor the only sound in the hushed silence.

Meg felt sick. Her body was rigid with tension, her nails biting deep into her palms, drawing blood and she felt the taste of nausea in her mouth as her stomach churned. She wanted to scream, to beg Simon to go back, but she had to keep silent to avoid destroying his concentration. Their lives depended on his driving, but each curve brought a new horror. Finally, Meg dropped her head and closed her eyes.

'Something wrong?' Simon asked smoothly.

'What happens if we meet another car?' she gasped.

'What's the matter? You aren't afraid, are you?' He sounded amused.

At that moment, she hated him. 'Deathly,' she snapped.

'Of heights?'

'No, of road accidents. I was in one when my stepmother was killed. I have been afraid ever since. I think I would die of fright if I had to drive this car.'

'Really? How interesting,' he drawled slowly, his velvety voice savouring her words. 'Well, you have nothing to fear. We won't meet another car. These tracks were made by the Jeep and a couple of trucks that hauled things up to the house last week. It hasn't snowed since.' He glanced through the windshield and grimaced. 'Until now.' Some fat, lazy snowflakes were drifting lazily and hitting the windshield.

'Does that mean we have no neighbours?' Meg asked.

'Yes. We're the only people crazy enough to spend the winter up here.'

She stared at him desperately. 'Then why must we? The whole winter, I mean.'

'Simple, my sweet. Once we're up here, we can't get down. After this snowstorm, the road will be impassable until spring.'

No wonder the man had looked at them as though they were crazy! But Simon had known this all along— he had heard the forecast predicting a snowstorm lasting three or four days. 'You didn't tell me!' she cried. 'You let me think it would be only for our honeymoon—for two weeks!'

'Don't you think our honeymoon will last longer than two weeks?' he mocked.

He had done it deliberately, for some cruel purpose. She knew it in her bones. But it was too late now to do anything about it, and the last thing she wanted to do was quarrel with Simon on their wedding day.

'What if one of us becomes ill?' she asked weakly.

'There's a telephone. Or if the lines are down, a short wave to the ranger station. They can send a helicopter in a real emergency. Any more questions?' When she said nothing, he added, 'You can look up now. We're almost there.'

Meg looked up. Ahead was a modern looking A-frame house, gleaming with windows and gay with bright paint. It was backed up cosily against the mountain side. With the snow falling, it looked like an Alpine Christmas card.

Meg drew a deep breath of relief. 'Oh, it's charming! I like it, Simon.'

'Sorry to disappoint you, darling, but that's our neighbour's house—when he's there. Our place is up the hill.' The road zigged and he swung the Jeep hard to the left. 'This is *our* place.'

There were no trees to soften the bald outline of the house standing in bleak isolation on top of the mountain, a lonely looking barn behind it. The road in front was churned with tyre tracks that were fast being covered with snow, and Simon pulled up close to the porch. He got out first and began briskly unloading luggage and boxes, stacking them on the sagging porch. Meg got out more slowly. The icy wind hit her with the force of a gale, almost knocking her backwards. She stumbled across the ice-coated ruts and stared at the place Simon had chosen for their first home.

It was an old house and had been built to last of weathered grey stone that had withstood the winter winds for years. But not even the falling snow could soften its stark ugliness.

'This place was built in the twenties.' Simon's breath smoked on the cold air. 'When my sister and I were little, my mother would bring us here for the summer to stay with our grandparents. It was never anything but a summer home, even in their day. A caretaker in town has been seeing to its maintenance for us.'

Nothing he was saying made any sense to Meg, but she picked up a suitcase and prepared to follow him into the house. As she opened the door, they were met by a rush of stale, freezing air that made her immediately question the reliability of the furnace. Simon turned on a light, and the naked bulb in the ceiling showed her a depressingly dark, dreary hallway covered with worn, cracked linoleum. The door slammed behind them, disturbing dust balls in the corners that rolled towards them like menacing tumbleweeds.

Simon preceded her into the next room, snapping on more lights. He moved about briskly, whipping dust sheets off the furniture and touching a match to the fire.

Meg dropped the suitcase and stared in disbelief. This was what had been called a parlour in her grandmother's day, and it was furnished with ugly monstrosities from the twenties. There was a davenport, its leather upholstery cracked with age, some stiff wooden armchairs, a wind-up Victrola and lamps covered with tasselled shades. Even the fireplace was small and stingy with a narrow mantel. At either end was a brass candlestick holding a melted blob of grey wax. Everything was dusty, and there was an unpleasantly musty odour in the air.

'Want to see the kitchen?' Simon asked brightly.

Meg trudged behind him silently, prepared for anything. The first sight that met her eyes was an old-fashioned, wood-burning stove.

'Don't worry,' Simon said soothingly. 'I brought along a campstove until you get the hang of it.'

The rest of the kitchen looked as though it had been transported straight from the ark. There was an elderly refrigerator, a single sink, and a dresser that was apparently used to hold dishes. There were no cabinets and the pots and pans hung from a rack above the stove. A large table, covered with yellowing newspapers and upended canning jars, was pushed against the wall.

The kitchen smelled of long ago meals and cold, stale air. Meg shuddered.

'We're going to have a little problem with the furnace,' Simon said apologetically. 'I don't want to worry you, but it's old and cranky, and I was advised to keep the thermostat low—just enough to keep the pipes from freezing. So, I'm afraid we're going to depend upon fires for heat. But we won't mind, will we, darling? There's plenty of firewood and coal and there's nothing nicer than an open fire.' He looked around nostalgically. 'I can remember my grandmother making bread at that old table. Can you make bread, Meg?'

'No,' she said repressively.

'There may be a recipe book around here somewhere.' He sounded cheerful. He opened the refrigerator door, then closed it hastily, but not before Meg saw that it was covered with a layer of green mould. 'It may need a little cleaning,' he said blandly, meeting her eyes.

Meg stared at him dazedly. She was so tired that she felt light-headed and her jaws ached with a compulsion to yawn. Furthermore, she was scared. Simon had changed. Had she married a man with some sort of primitive living complex? If so, it was up to her to work it out with him. She loved him, for better or worse. She gave him a wavering smile.

'I don't mind, Simon. Honestly.'

A fleeting look of something oddly like chagrin crossed his face, but he merely asked, 'Want to see the rest of the house?'

'Not if it's as bad as this.' She tried to make a joke out of it. 'Let's get the things in before it gets too dark.'

'I'll do that, darling,' he said gently. 'You find the room where you want to sleep. The bedrooms are upstairs.'

That cheered Meg up so she left the kitchen. On impulse, she tried a door at the end of the hallway behind the stairs, and discovered a bedroom with an adjoining bath. For a wonder, it was comparatively clean. The narrow single bed had been made up with fresh sheets and blankets and was spread with a patchwork coverlet. She recognised Simon's typewriter on a table in the corner.

'Found your room?' he asked softly behind her.

She turned, her face confused. 'This would be all right but it only has a single bed.'

'There's a double bed upstairs,' he said helpfully.

'I hope it's aired,' she said doubtfully.

'No problem,' he said easily. 'I bought new bedding for both rooms last week. I put your things in the bigger bedroom but you decide which you want. I tell you what, go look it over and I'll get supper after I put the Jeep in the barn. But only tonight, I warn you. After this, meals are your responsibility!'

Meg was smiling as she went upstairs and when she saw the front bedroom, she felt better. It wasn't so bad. Her luggage was already in it, the bed had been made with sheets and an electric blanket. Of course, the room was rather cheerless without curtains and a rug, but it wasn't as dirty as those downstairs. Once it was dusted and swept, she could sit in that rocker before a cheerful fire and even like this room.

There was a smaller bedroom across the hall and a narrow set of stairs leading to a bolted attic door. And the bathroom. Meg almost backed out of the bathroom after seeing it, but she forced herself to clean it with the scouring powder and sponge that had been left on the tub. Fortunately, there was plenty of hot water and an electric heater that *worked*. Standing shivering before the blessed warmth, she decided the bathroom might even get to be her favourite room.

She dressed in one of her caftans, the low-cut sexy one, then took Simon's gift out of her case before going downstairs. Simon had set a table in front of the fire, which was burning brightly now. Meg sat down and put the gift at his place as he brought in a tray of soup and sandwiches in paper plates and bowls.

'What's that?' he demanded.

'Your wedding present.' She was taken aback by his frowning look. 'It's just a little thing,' she added hastily, opening the box herself and taking out the paperweight. 'I thought it was rather pretty—and you could use it on your desk to hold your papers——' She stopped at the look on his face.

'You were premature,' he said harshly. 'The situation doesn't call for an exchange of gifts between us.'

She flushed. 'B-but I wanted ... You gave me my diamond ring.' She was stammering slightly. 'And you paid for my clothes——'

'Those things were bought for a purpose,' he replied cruelly. 'The ring was part of the other trappings of marriage and the clothes were necessary if you weren't to freeze up here this winter.'

We're quarrelling! Meg realised with dismay as she sought feverishly for a way to get back on the old footing. 'W-w-well, I like them, anyway, whatever the reason for you buying them,' she said quickly, giving him a bright, meaningless smile. 'I like our b-bedroom, too.'

'*Your* bedroom,' he corrected her flatly. 'I will occupy the one downstairs.'

She stared at him wordlessly, her mind shrinking away from the blunt meaning of what he had said. His face wore a cold, hard look. All day, that same look had kept her on edge. She hadn't understood it. Now, she knew why her instincts had told her something was wrong—there was no mistaking the look of dislike.

'What are you saying, Simon?' Her mouth was dry and brackish with the taste of fear. 'I ... d-don't understand.'

'You understand. You are not a fool, Meg.' He eyed her remotely. 'In a nutshell, I have no intention of consummating our marriage, nor of sharing a marriage bed with you. Not now, not ever. It wasn't an easy decision to make, for I'll admit, you turn me on. But not enough, my dear. Not nearly enough for the self-disgust I would feel afterwards.'

A coldness descended on Meg that went straight through the shrinking flesh to her heart, a heart that seemed to have shrivelled into a tiny, hard knot. She didn't want to hear any more but she knew Simon had no intention of sparing her. Somehow, she managed to keep her voice and eyes steady. For some reason, it was important that he not guess what he was doing to her.

'Why did you marry me, then, Simon? I think you'd better tell me the truth now.'

He laughed harshly. 'I gave it to you when I told you my name, but in your total self-absorption, it made no impression on you, did it?'

Meg frowned slightly, a memory teasing at the edge of her consciousness. 'Melton? Why should it?'

'Why should it, indeed? You couldn't be expected to remember the name of my sister, whose life you destroyed, then cold-bloodedly forgot,' he agreed savagely.

'*Your sister?* You're mad, Simon, I don't even know your sister. I——'

'She meant such a little to you that even now, you can't recollect the name of your victim. Think, my dear wife, about the innocent, sick girl whose husband you deliberately seduced and then killed, by driving his car over an embankment. And then, as if that wasn't enough, having destroyed her reason for living, her only happiness, the man she loved, you denied your guilt and claimed he was at fault! She took her own life because you'd made her too unhappy to live. Which makes you responsible for two deaths, not one, you amoral little bitch!' His voice lowered to a vicious snarl. 'You killed them both—Tony Hardwick and his wife, Barbara Melton Hardwick!'

CHAPTER FIVE

'Oh, God, no!' she cried piteously.

She put her hands up to her face as though to ward off a blow, but he gripped them between strong, merciless fingers and forced them into her lap. With despairing eyes, she stared into a face twisted into a mask of hatred. He spoke slowly, with cruel deliberation.

'Listen to me, you little cheat, and listen to me well for I won't say it but once. It soils the memory of my sister to speak her name in your presence, but I want you to know why I brought you here. Barbara left a letter for me. It wasn't the sort of letter a man likes to read from a beloved sister.' For a moment, a look of anguish twisted the hard, implacable features. 'She told me why she committed suicide. A red-haired young woman, beautiful, named Margaret Somers, came into her house in the guise of a companion and deliberately seduced her husband. Tony was a weak man with a sick wife, and he had his flings, which Barbara accepted because she loved him.' His mouth curled with contempt. 'But this time, Barbara was forced to watch the whole sordid affair unfold before her eyes, for you made sure she understood what was happening.' Meg, closing her eyes in agonised protest, could well imagine Carol doing just that. 'Barbara, chained to her home, had to endure your taunts, your attempts to humiliate her. The final blow came that last night. Tony had refused to marry you; Barbara had discharged you; and you returned to the house, drunk and disorderly. You demanded Tony marry you because you were pregnant. It destroyed Barbara, who had never been able to give him the child he wanted.'

'*No*, no,' Meg moaned helplessly. 'Please let me explain, Simon. I——'

He continued remorselessly as though she hadn't spoken. 'You flung yourself out of the house, hysterically threatening an abortion, and naturally, Tony followed you. Barbara heard the car driving away, and the way it screeched down the drive, she knew you were the one driving. What happened to your baby?' His eyes were cruel with mockery. 'Did you abort it later? Or *did it ever exist*? Either way, it served its purpose for Barbara did not want to go on living, knowing that somewhere in the world another woman was carrying Tony's child.'

'Simon, please listen to me!' Meg begged frantically. She fought to reach him, to touch him, shaking in her desperate effort to make him understand. 'Listen, Simon, I didn't do it, I tell you! Please let me explain what happened . . .!'

He struck at her hands violently. 'I know the official version was that he was driving,' he went on harshly. 'But the police didn't believe it, and neither did Barbara. And I don't, either! So stop trying to protest you're innocent! Tony was a good driver, and he had made that curve too many times, drunk and sober, to miss it the way he did that night! The police couldn't prove it because by the time they found you, you'd sobered up and swore up and down that Tony was driving the car.'

'No, I didn't,' she sobbed. 'I deliberately refused to give my oath—— I was careful about that. I said I—I blacked out but that was because I—I didn't want to perjure myself. Please, if you'll let me explain——'

'It sounds like you already have,' he commented ironically. 'Congratulations, that was a clever dodge, to claim you blacked out. No one could prove it wasn't true, could they? And it let you keep your skirts clean. Just what did happen? Or do you even know? You've told so many lies, I doubt if you do.'

'*No!*' She slammed her fist flat on the table, forcing herself to look into his black, hate-filled eyes. 'You *must* believe me, Simon! I didn't do it, I tell you! Not any of it! If you'll just give me a chance to explain, I'll——'

'If you continue to lie to me,' he said deliberately, 'I won't be responsible for what I do to you. We're all alone in this house and I assure you, I shall enjoy punishing you.' As she stared in appalled silence, he added rigidly, 'I don't think you realise just how much I despise you. I see Barbara every time I look at you——' He stopped and a look of unbearable pain contorted his features. 'She was beautiful and good, and you killed her! *You!* You selfishly crashed into her life and destroyed it!'

Meg buried her face in her hands, knowing that whatever she suffered, Simon was feeling a greater pain. Apparently, for her to continue protesting her innocence, added to his anguish. And, of course, he assumed she was protesting that she wasn't the driver of the car.

Meg ached to comfort him. He wasn't a violent man, nor did he enjoy hurting people. She knew that instinctively. Yet, he had threatened her—an act that must be abhorrent to his nature. Perhaps later, he would be willing to listen to her but for now, the best thing she could do was try to defuse his anger. Whatever he said to her and about her now didn't matter anyway, for her future was already smashed, her hopes and dreams in shambles.

She raised her head. 'How did you find me?' she asked dully.

'You remember Selby, don't you?' When she nodded, he added, 'He is a detective. All it took was your name, a description and your social security number. He traced you to Jacksonville within a couple of weeks. Great things, social security numbers.' He smiled cynically.

'Then, when you called Helen Rogers——'

'I already knew all about you and I tailored my job description to fit you.' Sardonically, he watched her reaction, then laughed shortly. 'You turned out to be quite a surprise. I thought you'd be a little tart on the make, whom I'd find easy to bully. Instead, you were different from Tony's usual choice in girls. You were older, for one thing, and intelligent... On the other hand, you had to be something special to make him forget Barbara's lovely money. I wondered about that, too, but finally decided the two of you had worked out some sort of plan to relieve her of a large share of it.'

'Simon...'

'I don't want to know any of the details,' he interrupted brutally. 'They're unimportant in the light of what happened. And I'm fully aware of your resourcefulness. Look at the roles you played for me, beginning that first day: the cool, efficient secretary, repulsing a pass; the innocent virgin—even the warm-hearted companion. Tony never had a chance, did he?' he added cynically.

'It was not an act!'

He ignored her. 'You had me puzzled from the beginning. For a while I thought of seducing you, then leaving you high and dry. It would have been easy enough, for you were begging to be taken.'

Meg's face flamed with colour, but she met his eyes bravely. 'What changed your mind?' she asked evenly.

'I saw it would be no punishment for a hardened little tramp like you. A woman who has had dozens of men would not be destroyed by a callous seduction.'

Meg flung up her head defiantly. 'If you feel that way, why did you marry me?'

'I almost didn't. That last night in St Augustine, if you had come to me and completed your humiliation, I might have been satisfied. But a smart girl like you wouldn't have been that obvious.' He observed her heightened colour sardonically. 'You were playing for marriage.'

'But you weren't. So why did you marry me?' she repeated painfully.

He smiled slowly. 'Why do you think?'

She flinched, staring at him in growing horror, unaware that her face was faithfully mirroring her thoughts. Had she been wrong about his capacity for violence?

He snorted impatiently. 'Oh, not that!' he said contemptuously. 'Get it out of your head that I intend rape. Or wife-beating. In fact, if you're a good girl and do as I say, I won't even lay a finger on you. When you go back down this mountainside in the spring, you'll still be the intact virgin you pretend to be,' he added sarcastically. 'But before that happens, I intend to teach you a lesson, my dear. You put my little sister through hell—I am going to do the same to you. Unfortunately, it won't equal Barbara's agony, but it will be hell on earth to a woman like you. That's why I married you, for only as my wife could I bring you here.'

'Here?' She looked around the room with dull incomprehension, then her face changed, filled with fear. 'Oh, God, are you going to leave me here alone all winter?'

He laughed with genuine amusement, then sobered at the terrorised look on her face. 'Don't be a damned fool! I may dislike you intensely, but I know you couldn't survive up here alone.' Then, as though that confession had cost him something, he added roughly. 'Leave you? No. It wasn't my plan to deny myself the pleasure of watching you struggle with this house.'

She swallowed her relief. 'Your plan?'

He surveyed her thoughtfully. 'So far, you've put up a good front, but I had the words of Barbara and a couple of her servants who gave me a true picture of Margaret Somers. She was a lazy little slut who didn't like hard work; was fond of her own skin; and seemed to need sex on a regular basis.' To her gasp of shock, he added impersonally, 'I've already explained that you won't get the latter from me. As for the other, you'll have plenty of work and no doubt, your pretty soft skin will suffer. This house, as you see, is in bad shape.' He looked around with relish. 'It is going to have to be cleaned in order to be inhabitable. *You* will be doing that cleaning. I will keep you supplied with firewood and coal, but you will have to do the rest. In other words, if you eat, you will have to cook on that stove in the kitchen. If you keep warm, you will have to keep the fires going. And you will be thrown on your own resources to keep from going mad from loneliness these long winter nights. I intend to stay busy writing my novel and I don't want to see anymore of you than is necessary.'

Meg's bludgeoned senses did not really take in what he was saying. Only one thing had touched her.

'Your novel. Was that all a lie, then?'

He looked at her coolly. 'I type as well as you do, my dear. Those sketches of yours, although attractive, were not necessary. My book locale is South America, not Florida. I needed an excuse to bring you to me, and I used that.' He indicated her food. 'Perhaps you'd better eat before it gets too cold.'

'I'm not hungry.'

He shrugged. 'Suit yourself. However, you might as well know this is the last meal I prepare, and the last fire I shall make except for the one in my own room. You won't freeze, for there are plenty of blankets, but I assure you, you will be very uncomfortable without a fire. I suggest, for now, you get a good night's sleep so you can work tomorrow.'

He turned and strode out of the room. Meg heard the door to his room slam and she wondered if he would eat *his* supper with a good appetite.

She sat on in the chair, too apathetic to move, and the tears came, big, silent tears at first, rolling down her pale cheeks, then great, tearing sobs that racked her slender frame. She hadn't cried in years, not since Alice died and left her with a burden too heavy for her young shoulders. She had carried it until Carol betrayed her, but she hadn't cried even then. Instead, she had squared her shoulders and soldiered on, the way people must when life disappoints them. But this was different. This was death. She had loved and been joyously happy: she had held her face up to the sun and dared to hope again. But death had put an end to her dreams, the death of her love. She had known when she fell in love with Simon that this was a once in a lifetime thing with her. By making her fall in love with him and then betraying her, Simon had destroyed her.

When there were no more tears left, she lay in the chair staring with desolate eyes at the dying fire. She was going to have to leave here as soon as the snow stopped, of course. She could not stay on, day after day, seeing the hatred in Simon's eyes, enduring his contempt and anger. But right now, she was too tired to think about it. Simon was right—she should go to bed.

She rose wearily to her feet, her emotional excesses leaving her weak and drained. Something hard and solid rolled to her feet and she looked down at the paperweight glittering among the folds of her gown. Her wedding present to Simon. The present he had spurned. Moved by revulsion, she picked it up and flung it into the fireplace, where she heard it give a satisfying crack as it scattered the ashes. Then, she turned and went to her bed upstairs.

It was a long time before she slept, and when she woke, she saw that her windows were filled with a strange, odd light. For a few minutes, her tired brain grappled with the reason for it before she saw it was snow.

'Get up!'

Meg cringed away from the voice that, even in her sleep, spelled hurt and pain. Then a rough hand was laid on her shoulder and she was shaken awake. Her eyes were sticky and swollen, but she managed to glare sullenly at the fully dressed figure who, booted legs apart, hands on hips, stood over her bed. His eyes narrowed on her swollen face.

'It looks like you cried all night!' he observed callously. 'A futile exercise, my dear. I am not moved by tears. Now, get up and get started on your work.' When she said nothing, he added, 'I've been outside and it's still snowing. The weather report says we can expect two more days of it. For this morning, only, I've cleaned the ashes out of the fireplace in the parlour and made coffee. But after that, I expect my meals promptly. Is that understood?'

She nodded spasmodically. She was trembling so violently she couldn't have spoken if her life depended on it. After observing her a moment or two longer, he turned away and walked out.

She drew a long, shuddering breath, hating him, vowing to make him sorry. Did he really think she would stay on and live with him in this awful place, making fires and cooking his meals, after the way he had spoken to her? If he wanted a slave, let him hire one! She was getting off this mountain just as soon as it stopped snowing, even if she had to walk, and there wasn't anything he could do about it, short of holding a gun to her head!

For starters, she had no intention of getting up on his orders! She lay there, burning with anger, while the shadows fell across the room and she dozed again. This time, the overhead light flashing in her eyes awakened her.

'Get up, you little cheat!' he commanded roughly. He yanked the blankets off her shivering body then, gripping her by the shoulders, hauled her out of bed. She swayed on her feet. 'You're not going to lie there and starve yourself to death!' If Meg's ears had been attuned to his voice, she would have caught the muted note of anxiety. 'You're going downstairs and eat if I have to ram it down your throat myself, do you hear?' He laid rough hands on her shoulders and started marching her across the room. She had just enough time to slip her feet into the shoes she had worn last night before he had her out of the room and going down the steps.

They went through the darkened parlour and into the room he had taken as his own. In contrast to the chilled dampness in the rest of the house, it was warm, cheerful and cosy. A fire burned brightly in the grate, and there was a delicious aroma of food in the air. Meg saw that the table that had held his typewriter was now set for two, and a bubbling casserole on a trivet occupied the centre of it. There was also a foil package of rolls and a pot of coffee. He pushed her into one of the chairs and she sat where he had put her, determined not to betray a single emotion.

'You can see, my dear wife,' he went on ironically, 'that I can take care of myself. In case you had any idea of trying to starve *me* to death, I am perfectly capable of cooking a meal, building a fire, or doing any of the other tasks I have assigned to you. I have allowed you one day to sulk but starting tomorrow, I expect you to work. If you don't,' he added deliberately, 'I have spent too many years among primitive cultures not to notice that a little judiciously applied corporal punishment works wonders with a balky wife.'

'You wouldn't dare!' Meg breathed in horror.

'Wouldn't I?' he asked reflectively. 'Just try me.'

'And you just try me!' she shrilled. 'I'd get even! I'd make you sorry you were ever born! I can think of dozens of ways! Oh, how I hate you! And when I think how I once thought I *loved* you——'

THE WINTER HEART 85

He picked up a spoon and served her plate with a generous helping of food as though she hadn't spoken. 'Now, eat,' he said pleasantly. 'I don't mind you hating me. Much better that than to have you pretending to love me, as you've been doing for the past three months.'

Meg drew in a sharp hurt breath, his remark making her see how little he trusted her. Or ever had. She caught her lip firmly between her teeth, then said calmly, 'It was really rather stupid of you to cut off the heat. Childish, even. By turning down the thermostat, you're forcing yourself to work just as hard as I will be doing.'

'I presume you're referring to my chopping wood?' he replied, beginning his meal with every evidence of enjoyment. 'I don't mind doing that. It's good exercise. And this is the only fire I will be responsible for.' There was a wicked glint in his eyes as he added softly, 'You'll be coping with the kitchen stove.'

'So what?' She tilted her chin. 'I may have a little trouble at first, but I don't anticipate any real problem. After all, *women* have been using stoves like that one for generations.'

'Exactly my point,' he agreed smoothly. He looked up from his plate. 'Incidentally, in case you're tempted to adjust the thermostat, it's located in this room. Which I shall keep locked whenever I go out. And I have a key to the basement, where the furnace is located. Now, eat your dinner so you will have the strength to work tomorrow.'

She turned glittering eyes on him. 'I am not a donkey! And you don't really think you're going to keep me here, day after day, working for you, do you?' she demanded fiercely. 'Oh, you may be able to force me to work tomorrow and perhaps the next day, but as soon as this snow ends, I'm getting out of here! I'm leaving you and as soon as I get to Denver, I'm getting a divorce.'

'True. But obviously, you don't have a realistic picture of your present situation,' he drawled silkily. 'When it finishes snowing, the drifts will be too high for you to walk. You couldn't move the Jeep two feet without shovelling a path for it first, even if you were fool enough to brave that road. As I've said before, there is *no* way off this mountain until the snow melts in the spring.'

'Then I'll hitch a ride on a snowplough!' she snapped. 'I certainly don't intend to stay here until spring and take your abuse!'

He smiled wolfishly. 'Snowplough?' He raised his eyebrows. 'Don't you listen to what I say, Florida girl? The snowploughs don't come up this mountain road.' His smile broadened as the truth finally hit her. 'I assure you.'

She remembered something he had said yesterday, when she had asked him what to do about illness. 'The telephone!' She looked around and her eyes fell upon a telephone beside the bed.

'By all means,' he said softly. 'But you'll find it out of order. Apparently, the storm has knocked it out. But in case that is a temporary condition, you won't be allowed to use the telephone. Make no mistake about that.'

Her mouth twisted with bitterness. 'And I suppose you have the short wave hidden away in here somewhere, too?'

'Let's just say you won't be allowed to get your hot little hands on it. Accept it, my dear, you're immobilised until I choose to let you go.'

She bit her lip but said nothing. She new in her bones that Simon would not put himself on this mountain top without a way off and it was up to her to find it. But she wasn't going to do it this way. She was going to have to be cunning, exercise a little guile. And she was going to have to keep up her strength so that she would be ready when she saw her chance. Picking up her fork, she began to eat, forcing down as much food as possible. When her throat absolutely refused to swallow another bite, she stood up and in dead silence, left the room.

The next morning, she rose before dawn. Downstairs, the kitchen was just as clammy and filthy as it had looked by the weak light of an electric bulb the other night. Added to that was the mess made by Simon when he had cooked on the campstove. Meg looked around grimly, then rolled up the sleeves of two sweaters and a flannel shirt. The first thing to do was to get the stove going and fortunately, there was plenty of hot water. She tinkered with the damper, then lit a sheet of newspaper and watched it go up the chimney stack with a satisfying roar. So. It was safe to build a fire in the fire box. Meg knew next to nothing about building fires, but she hoped that half remembered Girl Guide lore would come to her rescue. Starting with kindling stacked in the woodbox, then gradually adding firewood, she soon had a snapping little fire going. Later, she would add coal for heat. While the stove was warming up, she wiped it down with a soapy rag, then applied a can of blacking she found on a shelf above the sink.

'Well, Stove, it looks like you're a lady. So-o-o, I'm counting on you to help me wipe the smirk right off that man's smug face,' she murmured, stepping back and holding her blackened hands straight out. 'It's just you and me, pal, against the male world.'

The stove was warming up fast, so Meg took off her sweaters and hung them on the back of a chair. She was beginning to get hungry and regain a little of her confidence. Surely, she thought, as she scoured the washing-up bowl, then dumped all the pots and pans into soapy water, there was something she could do to show Simon the truth. Of course, he had been hurt by his sister's suicide, and he thought she was to blame, but if she could get him to really listen to her, then wouldn't things get back to normal? Even if normal meant a friendly divorce, which was about the best she could hope for now. At any rate, it was worth a try.

By eight o'clock, Meg had the kitchen scrubbed, including the floor. The pots hanging on their rack were shining. She had unearthed some dishes in a blue willow pattern and had them ranged along the clean shelves of the dresser. 'Stove' was basking with warmth and she had put an iron skillet over an open eye and filled it with strips of bacon. The coffee pot was scenting the air with its aroma and biscuits were baking in the oven.

Simon walked in, in the midst of it all, looking surly and sleepy-eyed.

'Good morning,' she said breezily. 'How about some breakfast?'

He looked around in amazement.

She smiled. 'Eggs? Biscuits? Butter? Jam? I've been busy and found the food you put in the pantry. Sit down and I'll have your breakfast ready in a jiffy.'

He sat down warily and she smiled secretly to herself. It was going to be easier than she thought. The way to a man's heart *was* through his stomach and while Simon was eating, she was going to make him listen to her.

Putting a plate of bacon and eggs before him, she poured orange juice and coffee before sitting down with her own plate. She sipped her coffee nervously and as he started to eat, she began talking.

'Simon, I know how you feel and that you asked me not to refer to this again, but even a criminal before the bar gets a chance to plead his case, doesn't he?'

'Go on,' he growled.

'Well, I want to explain what *really* happened in Miami.' And taking a deep breath, she began telling him about how Carol had used her social security card and name because of the shoplifting charge; how she had come home that night, shaken and weeping, and hysterically forced Meg to take the blame for Tony's death. She told him about Pierre and how he could prove that what she was saying was the truth. Then, she told him why she had left Miami, after Carol walked out on her. He listened without a change of expression, eating steadily, and she couldn't tell from his face if he believed her or not. Finally, she finished and waited breathlessly.

He pushed his cup forward for her to pour him a second cup of coffee, then leaned back in his chair and looked at her, a trace of sardonic amusement in his eyes.

'You know, one of the first things that repelled me about you was your indifference to your little stepsister. It was too much like your callous attitude towards Barbara. You see, I had had Paul Selby look into your background so I knew all about her before I saw her picture in your room. I knew she was just a kid, yet you'd apparently abandoned her and left town.'

'Not abandoned her. She——'

'Hush,' he said with soft menace. 'Let me talk. You've had your turn, and now, it's mine. Not that it hasn't been a great fairy tale,' he added sarcastically. 'Put to music, it might even make the charts. I guess you've had all day and a couple of nights to think about it, and you've come up with the idea of blaming it all on an innocent kid. It was worth a try, anyway, and if I had been the kind of fool Tony was, I might have believed every word of it. You mentioned your old boss, who could back you up, and I'm tempted to have Selby talk to him just to prove you're bluffing, but— why bother? No one but an idiot would believe that every policeman and reporter in Miami fell for a case of mistaken identity, dreamed up, not by an expert, but an eighteen-year-old kid! You give yourself away every time you turn around. That terror the other day when we were driving up here, for instance. Now, that was real—but it had nothing to do with an old accident. It reminded you of the night Tony was killed, didn't it? It scared you so you'll never venture down the mountain on your own.' The twisted smile he wore didn't quite reach his eyes, and Meg saw she had been a fool to imagine she could change Simon's mind about her. He was too biased, too stubborn to listen to her without prejudice.

'It occurs to me to wonder why you've made up this elaborate story for my benefit,' he went on softly. 'Last night, you were breathing fire and swearing you were going to get off this mountain, come hell or high water.' The dark eyes iced to a glacial silver and the sensual mouth hardened. 'Now, you've changed your tune. So I can only assume you've had second thoughts, and realising you're stuck with me for the winter, are desperate to make me accept you as an innocent victim.' He rose with deliberate slowness and pulled her to her feet. Huge and terrifyingly masculine, he loomed over her shrinking figure. 'You've been without a man for days. I won't say weeks, for I'm sure you got your satisfaction while I was away from you in Jacksonville. But you wanted me badly those days in Denver.'

A humiliating tide of colour swept Meg's face. Simon knew her so well! And with the unerring aim of a master archer, he went straight for the jugular. She felt shamed, dirty, her innocent overtures of love made to seem like the slick sexual advances of a practised sensualist. She wanted to creep away somewhere and cry from the sheer pain of it. Her mouth began to tremble, and she gripped her lower lip firmly between her teeth and bit down savagely to stop the tears from falling.

Simon had been watching her closely and suddenly, with an inarticulate groan, he pulled her into his arms. He began to kiss her fiercely, his mouth tasting the blood on her maltreated lip. To her horror, Meg met him with a wild, abandoned eagerness that she would remember later with shame and loathing. His hand roamed over her breasts and she couldn't control the treacherous hardening and swelling as they responded to his experienced caresses. And when he tried to release her, she clung to him with a frantic urgency that betrayed her hunger.

'It's true, isn't it?' he demanded thickly. 'I could take you right now, and you would glory in having got what you wanted!'

She jerked away and began crying weakly. Her body tensed, desperately trying to fight the betraying shudders.

'Stop crying!' he snarled with a sort of baffled fury. 'I said I wouldn't touch you and I won't! You're allowed one mistake and you've had it. Just don't try to give me another fairy tale because you want a man in your bed. When I want you, I'll take you, but it will be in my own good time. And I'm going to have to feel a lot less choosy than I do right now!' he added with deliberate cruelty.

He walked out, leaving her to pick up the pieces. She had learned her lesson. It had been a hard one, but never again, she vowed, would she try to get Simon Egan to listen to her explanation.

CHAPTER SIX

AFTER that, Meg stopped trying to get Simon to believe her. He was too filled with hatred and bitterness and she no longer cared. She knew he wouldn't believe her even if Carol herself told him the truth. And that was a laugh. Thinking of Carol and the way she had twisted the truth, and yet got away with it, made Meg wonder about life's little ironies.

The snowstorm lasted another three days, with the drifts piling up past the windows on the north side of the house, and the wind howling around the corners by day and night. The first morning it stopped, a feeble sun came out and Meg heard Simon outside, chopping wood. When he came in, covered with snow, he told her harshly to get her outer clothing on and come outside. She obeyed him without a word, and the first thing she did, after leaving the covered back porch where the firewood was kept stacked, was to sink into snow to her waist.

Simon dragged her out with callous ease and deposited her roughly on the porch.

'You can go inside now,' he said curtly. 'I just wanted you to know what you'd be up against if you tried to leave the house. In front, you'd be in drifts over your head.' Grudgingly, he added, 'Later, I'll show you how to use snowshoes, but that will be after I'm sure you've got over this crazy idea about trying to get away.'

She noticed then for the first time that he was wearing something like tennis rackets attached to his boots but she said nothing as she stamped and brushed off the snow.

Back in the house, she watched intently from the

window, noting the odd, slinging motion Simon used to move his feet as he walked to the barn to check on the Jeep, then return. So, this was how one could get off the mountain! It seemed simple. All she had to do was wait for him to show her how to use them.

In the meantime, she worked, work she did not mind at all. Actually, it was a panacea to get her through the days and make her tired enough to sleep through the nights. Had everything been normal, and she had been making this a home for Simon, she would have even enjoyed it, for there was something satisfying about chasing dirt and cobwebs that hadn't seen a broom or mop for ten years. Of course, the house would always look ugly and bare without curtains or rugs, but Meg kept a fire in her room all the time, and she could forget the black staring windows as she lay in her bed at night and watched it flicker on the ceiling.

After the work became nothing more than routine housekeeping, boredom set in. It was the one taunt of Simon's that haunted her: she was afraid she would indeed go mad for lack of something to do. She had always been a busy person; now, she sat for long hours idle, listless. She hadn't touched a brush or pencil since leaving Florida. It was as though all creative urge had died in her. Simon's presence was the only thing that provoked a reaction in her, and that was fear.

Part of her unnatural apathy was due to the fact that she had had to abandon her escape plan. It had given her hope until the day Simon had her strap her feet into a pair of his boots and heavy snowshoes, then took her out to walk in them. She had been eager to learn but within a few minutes, the muscles of her calves were screaming with pain. Finally, her trembling legs wouldn't allow her to move. After that, Simon had had a satisfied air of triumph, as though he had proved his point, that there was no way she could go down a mountain in snowshoes.

She developed a fine drawn look from strain, loss of appetite and insomnia. She was a good cook and served appetising meals that Simon seemed to enjoy, but the day following the snowshoe episode, he noticed her slipping away as usual, to avoid having her meal with him.

'Come back here and sit down!' he called roughly.

She sat down with a nervous flash of green eyes. He studied her frowningly, his eyes noting the clean jeans and shirt and the severely braided hair before moving on to the pale face and shadowed, downcast eyes. His gaze sharpened on the trembling hands held tightly in her lap. He thought with a sudden surge of compunction that she looked like a whipped child, then was savagely angry with himself for feeling pity.

'From now on, you're eating your meals with me,' he said coldly. 'I don't want you to slip away like you've been doing anymore. If you're trying to make yourself sick so I'll be forced to call a doctor, I can tell you now—it won't work! I'm perfectly capable of force feeding you, if necessary. So, if you don't want me in your room, forcing soup down your throat, you'd better pick up your appetite.'

Of course, he had guessed she was afraid of him and that his threat to invade her bedroom would be effective in making her eat. She had already realised that her own foolishness had put her into this situation. Because of her loneliness, she had been susceptible, for any other girl would have been suspicious of a fiancé who rationed his kisses and never spoke a word of love. She had had doubts herself, but because she was so starved for his love, she would not allow them to materialise. Now, she desperately needed the time and solitude to repair her shattered emotions.

One afternoon, as she sat gazing apathetically at her fire, she thought of the attic. There might be magazines up there she could read. She rose, feeling a faint flicker of excitement as she hunted for a flashlight. Unbolting the attic door, she found that it was dimly lit by dormer windows and even slightly warm from the chimneys. And it was not even very dusty. Meg wandered around, noticing the usual attic junk of broken furniture and rolled-up rugs. There were two steamer trunks that looked interesting. She opened the first one curiously and saw that it contained an assortment of women's clothing. Carefully, she held up a dress. The style and material was from the twenties and early thirties and the interior of the trunk smelled faintly of long ago lavender. The other trunk, redolent of mothballs, held bedspreads, curtains and linen sheets, thin and fragile with age. Meg's hands trembled with excitement as she lifted out each item. When she raised the sheets and saw what was beneath them, she let out her breath on a long gasp of pleasure. *Books!* She had longed for—craved—books! Old books they were, to be sure, of the *St Elmo* and *Beverly of Graustark* vintage—but oh, to have books again to read! She wouldn't have cared if they had been moralistic Victorian tales for children. Then, she almost laughed aloud. Speaking of the devil, here was *Pilgrim's Progress*! She opened it carefully and saw, in childish handwriting, the inscription, 'Lucy Thompson, 9 years old, February 10, 1901'.

Meg smiled, wondering if little Lucy was Simon's grandmother. If so, these clothes surely belonged to her.

Gathering the books hastily together, she crept downstairs like a thief and hid them in her suitcase. Then she returned for the bedspreads and curtains. When she had brought everything down to her room, she spread it all out on her bed and looked at it gloatingly. The red plush curtains with the tassels were just the thing for the parlour and she chose the faded rose chintz for her bedroom. The rest of the curtains she would return to the trunk.

Back in the attic, she re-opened the trunk of Lucy's

dresses. They were all summer dresses, made of good-quality material that one seldom saw nowadays. Materials like dimities, calicoes, muslins and cotton percales, with small, old-fashioned prints. Taken apart, she mused, they would make fine material for a quilt.

Meg, who had been kneeling beside the trunk, sat down suddenly, struck by an idea. Why not? She knew a little about quilt making, so why couldn't she use them to make her own quilt? They had lain in this trunk for fifty years without anyone touching them, so who would know, or care?

Of course, she told herself, she would have to be careful to keep it a secret from Simon, but that was no problem, since he never came to her room. And if she did succeed in making it, then later, when she got off this mountain and Simon was gone forever, wouldn't this quilt be something she could treasure as a memory? Not because he had almost destroyed her, but because she hadn't let him? In other words, a sort of symbol of her victory over Simon—and Carol, too. When she looked at her quilt, it would tell her that in spite of everything they had done to her, she hadn't broken. She laughed softly to herself, and her laughter was so rusty that her eyes widened in surprise. She must do it more often, before she forgot how.

She was gripped by sheer excitement as she gathered up the dresses to take to her room. At the bottom of the trunk was a box of buttons, embroidery thread and an embroidery hoop. She left them where they were.

She ate her dinner absently that night, her dreamy silence so different that Simon watched her suspiciously. As soon as she finished the dishes, she hurried back upstairs to the curtains. She ironed them first, then hung them, and stood back smugly to observe the effect. It closed out the night, and made a cheerful haven of her room.

Then, she sat in her rocker and planned her quilt on a

Open your heart to Love
with 12 Romances Free
your welcome gift from Mills & Boon

plus the exclusive Mills & Boon **TOTE BAG FREE**

Love, romance, intrigue...all are captured for you by Mills & Boon's top selling authors. By becoming a regular reader of Mills & Boon's romances you can enjoy twelve superb new titles every month plus a whole range of special benefits: your very own personal membership card, a free monthly newsletter packed with recipes, competitions, exclusive book offers and a monthly guide to the stars, plus extra bargain offers and big cash savings.

As a special introduction we will send you 12 exciting Mills & Boon Romances and an exclusive Mills & Boon Tote Bag FREE when you complete and return this card.

At the same time we will reserve a subscription to Mills & Boon Reader Service for you. Every month, you will receive twelve of the very latest novels by leading Romantic Fiction authors, delivered direct to your door. And they cost just the same as they would in the shops – postage and packing is always completely Free. There is no obligation or commitment – you can cancel your subscription at any time.

It's so easy! Send no money now – you don't even need a stamp. Just fill in and detach this card and send it off today.

FREE BOOKS CERTIFICATE

Dear Susan,

You're special introductory offer of 12 free books is too good to miss. I understand they are mine to keep with the Free Tote Bag.

Please also reserve a Reader Service Subscription for me. If I decide to subscribe, I shall, from the beginning of the month following my free parcel of books, receive 12 new books each month for £13.20, post and packing free. If I decide not to subscribe, I shall write to you within 10 days. The free books will be mine to keep, in any case.

I understand that I may cancel my subscription at any time simply by writing to you. I am over 18 years of age.

2A6T

Name _____
(BLOCK CAPITALS PLEASE)
Address _____

Signature _____

Postcode _____

Remember, postcodes speed delivery. Our special offer applies in UK only and is not valid to present subscribers. Mills & Boon reserve the right to exercise discretion in granting membership. Should a price change become necessary you will be notified in advance. Offer expires 30th June 1986.

To Susan Welland
Mills & Boon
Reader Service
FREEPOST
P.O. Box 236
CROYDON
Surrey CR9 9EL.

SEND NO MONEY NOW

NO STAMP NEEDED

sketch pad. She wanted to appliqué blocks of pictures, and it would have to be lap quilt, of course. She would make each block a picture of Lucy and early Colorado life. She just wished she knew more about her, Leadville, its old Opera House, the mines, and the brief spans of the silver millionaires. And this house on the top of the mountain. As a matter of fact, Lucy could be any child who was brought west by pioneering parents. And those buttons—some were unique. She thought wistfully of using one of the baby ones on a square for herself. It would be out of place, of course, but if the quilt was to be really personal, she could appliqué the house where she was born, with the orange tree in the back yard. It was the last place where she had been really happy.

She fell asleep pleasantly tired, her mind buzzing with ideas, and the following morning, she awakened early. Reaching under her pillow, where she had hidden it, she brought out *St Elmo*, and started reading it.

She put it aside reluctantly when it was time to go downstairs and begin Simon's breakfast. This morning, she served him pancakes and sausages and as he ate, he watched her speculatively.

Finally, he asked, 'Would you like to try another lesson on the showshoes this morning?'

'No, thank you,' she said sweetly.

'Does that mean you've given up your idea of escaping?'

Her eyelashes swept open in startled surprise. So she hadn't fooled him, after all! 'Are you asking me for a promise?' she asked tartly.

'No, because I wouldn't trust you even if you made it,' he said blandly. 'I merely wondered if you'd finally realised it would be insanity to try.'

'Yes,' she replied in dulcet tones. 'I am beginning to think you're right. I'm either going to have to wait it out, or *you* are going to become so bored you decide to call on the forest rangers.'

'Don't hold your breath,' he said drily.

As soon as Meg finished cleaning the kitchen and had banked Stove into a slow heat, with a pot of spaghetti sauce simmering on the back eye, she went to the attic to retrieve the box of buttons and embroidery skeins. The attic was much lighter by morning light and she noticed in a corner of pair of skis and showshoes, both of which she had missed earlier. She saw at once that the snowshoes were much smaller and lighter than Simon's.

She carefully locked the door of her bedroom before trying them on but she could tell that walking in them would be much easier. Simon was a devil! She blazed with anger. He had strapped her in lead weights, knowing she would become discouraged. And only this morning, he had taunted her about it! Did he know these were in the attic? No, she was sure of that, but she clutched the snowshoes to her breast, looking around desperately for a place to hide them. Finally, she slid them under the bed.

Even so, she thought, as she stared discouraged out of the window, she couldn't walk the ten miles down the mountain to the snowploughed road. And perhaps another additional twenty-five miles to Brennan's Pass, if no car came along. She might manage a mile or two but that kind of trek could only be accomplished by an experienced man. She was afraid of the snow. It was her enemy—she couldn't imagine anyone *ever* wanting to paint a snowscene. From here, it wasn't even a view, just a dreary landscape of white on white, with a faint trail of smoke curling above the snow-capped trees.

Smoke! Meg blinked. Smoke meant people and people meant hope! But where? Then she remembered the A-frame house below. Had Simon lied about it, too? Were there neighbours just down the road, less than a mile away? Here was her way out! She could walk those few hundred yards. If all went well, she could be out of here tomorrow!

She sat down, exulting, and applied herself to picking out the seams of Lucy's dresses. Could she take the quilt with her? Regretfully, she decided not to. She needed the space in her satchel for other things. It would have to be left for the second Mrs Simon Egan to make of it what she would. Blindly, Meg stabbed at a thread and drove the needle into her finger. She was a fool, she told herself bitterly, sucking her finger. Of course there would be a second Mrs Egan someday—and if she even gave a hint to Simon that the thought bothered her, he would take delight in bringing it up.

The next morning, she started off with optimism, having waited until Simon was safely at his morning stint with the typewriter. An hour later, within sight of the A-frame house, she began to wonder if she had been a fool. She had faced snowdrifts, the frozen surface of the snow that was slick as glass, and a wind so powerful it literally slammed her against the side of the mountain. But somehow, floundering, gasping, eyes streaming, remembering her snowshoe drill, she had managed to get this far, only to come to an exhausted halt and realise she couldn't move another step.

'I say, little fellow, can't you get going again?'

She had slumped weakly to the ground, and now, she looked up, her blurry eyes taking in a figure. Her exhausted brain assumed that Simon had found her, and she raised her arms towards the anonymous figure.

'Come on, sonny, let's make those legs work. You shouldn't have stopped to rest, you know. Sometimes your muscles seize up when you do that, especially if you aren't used to walking in showshoes.

'I'm not,' she snuffled.

'I can see that. Don't cry, I'm here. Luckily, I saw you from my window, and I'll get you inside if I have to carry you. You're little enough, aren't you?' He knelt and slung her across his back in a fireman's grip, then almost dropped her. 'Hey! You're a girl!'

'I know!' she gasped.

He laughed. 'Okay, little girl, let's get going!'

What a nice voice, she thought hazily. How kind he is! When they came to the house, he started up the outside stairs. 'I haven't got around to digging out downstairs yet, so we go in through the upper floor,' he explained.

On the upper porch, he put her down long enough to fumble with the glass door. Meg hung over the railing and looked down at the little car.

'What's that?' she panted.

'That? My snowmobile. How else do you think anyone gets up this mountain?'

Meg didn't answer. She had fainted.

CHAPTER SEVEN

WHEN she came to, she was lying on a mattress on the floor. She was wearing nothing but her blouse and panties and was packed in a cocoon of blankets. She looked around wonderingly. This was a sleeping loft, completely bare except for a couple of mattresses on the thickly carpeted floor, some swag lamps and a bookcase against one of the walls. There was a stairwell circle in the centre.

A worried face bent over her, a young, pleasant face, with a dusting of freckles across his nose, a wide mouth, blue eyes and a thatch of sandy hair. 'Hi!'

'Hi, yourself,' she said weakly. 'Who are you?'

'Chris Turner. Are you all right?' he added anxiously. 'I didn't expect you to faint but I caught you just before you hit the floor.' He flushed. 'I hope you don't mind, but I had to get those wet things off. They're in the drier. And I made some tea. Can you drink it if I go get it now?'

'Yes.' But when he started to rise, she stopped him, reluctant to break contact with the first friendly face she'd seen in a long time. 'You get plenty of sunlight here.' She glanced at the wall of glass.

'This place was built to trap solar energy. It stays warm all the time with just a fire downstairs. I understand the landlord is sort of a nut on the subject.'

'Then you don't own it?'

'No. I rented it through an agent for the Christmas season. I needed a place to write my thesis.'

'Christmas.' A wistful expression drifted across her face. 'I had forgotten about it. When *is* Christmas?'

'Say, where have you been, anyway?' he asked disbelievingly.

101

Instead of answering, she asked tentatively, 'Just before I fainted, I heard you say something about a—a——'

'A snowmobile,' he answered promptly. 'You saw it outside and asked me about it. How did you think I got here, anyway? This is a private road. The snowploughs don't come up here so there's no way of getting off the mountain.'

She smiled faintly. 'I know. Chris, can you take me to town?' Her voice was strained. 'Now, *today*? You don't have to stay. Just leave me there and you can come right back up.'

'Today?' He was obviously astonished. When she nodded, he said reluctantly, 'I suppose I could but—is it really urgent? I don't understand why——' he stopped, frowning. 'What's going on up there at the Egan place, anyway? Why can't you use their snowmobile?'

'My——' She stopped, sensing that Chris might be reluctant to help if he knew she was married. 'My—boyfriend—doesn't have one. We—we've quarelled and I want to leave. Will you take me?'

'What's your name?'

'Meg. Meg Somers. Will you take me, Chris?'

He looked uncomfortable, although she saw that she could persuade him if she put additional pressure on him. It certainly hadn't occurred to him that she was married. For one thing, she had taken off her rings the night of her wedding and left them on the dresser. Meg was thankful to be spared from telling the truth, for she shrank from exposing the sordid details of their marriage to anyone at all, much less a boy as naïve as Chris.

'All right,' he mumbled. 'But I won't leave you in Brennan's Pass. I'll take you on to somewhere else, where you can stay for the night.' He rose. 'I'll see if your things are dry.'

Meg didn't answer. She had slid into sleep.

She thought she was dreaming the high, keening sound of a buzz-saw, and opened her eyes bewilderedly to see that Chris was looking alarmed. The sound descended into a whine, then cut off abruptly.

'I'd better see who that is,' Chris muttered, diving for the stairs.

Meg half heard his words, but she didn't worry. Blissfully unaware of what it meant, she snuggled into the blankets and slept. She didn't hear the sound of the noisy scraping door or the voices, but she awakened when the booted feet pounded on the metal steps of the twisting staircase. She opened her eyes in time to see Simon's head appear in the opening, his hair ruffled from the wind. His face was taut with anger, his eyes almost black, and there was a ring of white around his compressed lips. He erupted from the stairwell with a muted roar of rage.

'You damned, stupid, harebrained little fool!' he stormed. 'What the hell do you mean, doing a dumb, stupid thing like that? You could have frozen to death out there in the snow! I didn't even discover you were missing until fifteen minutes ago, and I didn't know how long you'd been gone, how you'd got away—or *what* had happened! The snowshoes were still there—I couldn't believe, at first—and when I didn't see your tracks——! I didn't know anyone was living here, so I—! I could beat the hell out of you, scaring me like that!' All the time he was talking, he was pacing. He had ripped off his gloves and was slapping them between his palms as though that was the only way he could restrain himself from laying violent hands on her.

Meg shrank back against the pillow, jolted out of her exhausted slumber by the sheer violence of his presence. Then, as he talked, it dawned on her that he had no intention of touching her—most of his rage was a result of fear. She frowned and licked her dry lips, then said huskily, 'He has a snowmobile. He can get off the mountain.'

He went absolutely still, the only sign of reaction about him his eyes, which showed a flash of surprise, then smouldered with anger. 'So what?' he asked coolly. 'I have one, too. But you're not going anywhere but back to the house.'

Her eyes narrowed with calculation, and as though sensing her impulse to call for help, he leaned over her menacingly. 'If you try to involve that boy in what is between us, I'll not only kick him out of this house but I'll ruin him in this state.' He ground out his words between clenched teeth. 'Now, get up!' he added. 'We're getting out of here before you get any more ideas!' He ripped the blankets off, then stared at her half-naked body, his eyes narrowing until they were slits of rage. '*God*! So this is how you intended paying him! I noticed he looked as guilty as hell when he let me in. And you didn't even tell him you were married, did you?'

'Mr Egan! I have M-Mrs Egan's clothes here, out of the drier!' Chris was apparently on his way up.

Simon gave a low growl of fury. 'Stay down there!' he snarled, leaning over the stair rail. 'I'll come down and get them! Remember what I said,' he added over his shoulder to Meg, before taking the stairs two at a time on his way down.

Meg huddled shivering in the blankets. She was too tired and disoriented to think what to do. She knew she should do something about getting away while she had a possible ally, but Simon's threat had paralysed her. She couldn't let Chris become involved in her mess.

While she was trying to reason through the drugging mists of sleep, she heard Simon's gritty voice, 'I appreciate everything you've done, but I think I can dress my own wife, thank you.'

Chris's voice bleated some protest, and Simon answered, 'I'd believe you better if you had made some attempt to call me. We *are* on the 'phone line, you know.'

The next thing she knew, Simon was saying in a soft, low growl, 'If you don't, I'm going to have to put some snow down your back.'

'Wha-at?' She had been asleep again. She opened her eyes and stared into the face bending over her. The craggy lines had softened and there was even a muscle twitching at the corner of his mouth. 'I've done everything else,' he drawled, 'but I can't put your jacket on until you sit up.'

She looked around dazedly. She was still on the mattress and it was true, he had done everything but put on her jacket, ski mask and gloves. She pulled herself upright and obediently thrust her arms into her jacket then waited like a child until he zipped it up. She leaned against his shoulder while he put on the gloves and mittens and by the time he had finished, she was asleep again.

She awakened with the harsh wind in her face. She was strapped into a snowmobile and they were going up the hill towards the house. She moaned softly in protest, but the sound was lost in the keening whine of the motor.

She was still awake when Simon stopped at the back porch, where the snow had been shovelled away. He unloaded her over his shoulder like a sack of flour which he dumped on the porch, then drove the snowmobile towards the barn. Moving on rubbery legs, she made her way to the kitchen, where she got rid of most of her outer clothing. Her boots defeated her. She was feebly struggling with them when Simon came in.

'Would you like some sweet tea?' he asked, kneeling and pulling off her boots.

'I think I want to sleep,' she mumbled with a yawn.

'That's probably what you need most. Turner said you went out like a light as soon as you got there.'

'I thought I was supposed to be seducing him,' she muttered resentfully.

He didn't answer, and the next thing she knew, she was being carried upstairs to her room. Simon's wool shirt was scratching her face and she moved her head around, muttering irritably as she tried to find a comfortable spot. Finally, she found it against his neck where the warm brown skin was soft and throbbing gently against her cheek.

She was vaguely aware of Simon stripping off her slightly damp jeans and flannel shirt before slipping her into the bed. She moaned and shivered, her chilled flesh protesting violently against the cold sheets. She heard him crashing around, opening drawers, saying something about her nightgown. The he flipped the covers back. By that time, the electric blanket had begun to warm her and she struck at his hands, protesting at the invasion. He laughed.

'Oh, very well, then, if you want to sleep in the raw.' But even that deliberate provocation did not awaken her.

She heard him briefly at the fireplace, building up the fire, then the last thing she remembered, he was sliding something on her finger. His words reached her through the mists of sleep.

'This should clear the misconception in Turner's mind. And anyone else's, too, who might be interested.'

She was still trying to puzzle his meaning when she fell asleep.

She was dreaming, beautifully, a pleasurable dream, like nothing she had ever felt in her twenty-four years of life. She was back home in Florida, lying in a deliciously warm bed of sand, with the hot sun beating down on her and Simon stroking her skin, bestowing small, sweet kisses on her lips and eyelids and the sensitive areas behind her ears. His hands were exploring her body, stroking, feeling, exploring her warm throbbing flesh. The sensitive fingertips traced the outlines of her parted lips, the faint indentations at the base of her throat, then moved to the rounded flesh of her breasts, fondling them with an exquisite tenderness that had her sobbing, twisting and turning in her sleep. Still half asleep, her parted lips searched hungrily for his mouth and she was shocked awake at the feel of his answering kiss.

She was not dreaming. She was naked, lying in her own bed, with Simon lying opposite her, engaged in a thorough, sensual exploration of her body. He was naked also, and she realised that the sweet throbbing she had felt in her sleep was not altogether the arousal of her own body.

Their eyes met and she recoiled from the look of frank lust she glimpsed in the dark pupils. Their colour deepened as he watched the varying emotions cloud her face—at first, puzzlement, then shocked awareness, followed by a delicate tide of scarlet colour that covered her throat and mingled with the freckles on her nose.

'Wha-what do you think you're doing?' she croaked.

His eyes crinkled with amusement and briefly, his lips relaxed. 'Don't ask stupid questions, Red! Don't you remember? You were freezing and you practically forced me to get into bed with you to keep you warm.'

'I did not!' she gasped indignantly. 'I would have remembered if—you're lying! Get out of my bed!' she cried furiously.

'No way. Stop struggling, sweetheart. Relax and enjoy it.'

Appalled and infuriated by the cynical command, she started striking wildly at him with her hands and feet, but she only succeeded in bruising herself on the hard firmness of his body. Effortlessly, he captured her flailing hands and held them away from her body.

'Let me go!' she sputtered. 'You're out of line, you lying skunk! All the way!'

His hands tightened a little but he didn't move. 'Not on your life,' he said grimly. 'I've decided I'm collecting dues. I'm going to get a little of what you've been passing out so freely to all the other boys.'

She reddened with rage, her eyes spitting with the fury of green glass. 'You have a dirty, evil, little mind, Simon Egan, and it's matched by your lying, hypocritical promises! You said you wouldn't touch me! You—*promised*!'

The craggy cheekbones flushed slightly, but he didn't move. 'I didn't promise a damn thing. I merely said I didn't want you—then!' he drawled. 'I've changed my mind. It's going to be a long, hard winter, sweet, and we're going to be spending it together. As husband and wife. Don't tell me it isn't what you want—and need. You're already getting restless, and I find that living in close proximity with a sexy little piece like you is getting to me, so I'm cutting myself in on what's due me.'

'You sadistic, sarcastic, filthy-minded brute!' she spat. 'You're not cutting in on a damned thing, because I'm handing out *nothing*—not to *any* man and certainly not to the likes of you! You can't call me a trollop one minute and take advantage of the situation by raping me the next!'

'Who said anything about rape?' His lips quirked with enjoyment. 'You were ready for me awhile ago, so just relax and enjoy yourself—you'll be ready for me again.'

'*Never!* Not in a million years!' she raged. She started to struggle again, but found she couldn't move a muscle. 'Let me go!' she panted hoarsely.

He chuckled and she reacted with violence. Thrashing her head about furiously, rearing and bucking with rage, she fought wildly until she realised she was merely exhausting herself against his strength. She subsided weakly then, with a soft whimper of defeat. Moving with leisurely deliberation, he loosened her hands and pulled her firmly into his arms, then lowered his mouth on hers. Her long lashes swept her cheeks as she defeatedly allowed his kiss. His hands moved langourously on her body, smoothing and stroking, and it reacted with a treacherous softening and quickening that she was powerless to prevent.

'Look at me,' he muttered. 'I want to look into your eyes.'

Her lids parted with drugged slowness, disclosing green eyes filled with a liquid light. He gave a satisfied little grunt, then moved his hands with deliberation until she moaned.

He smiled. 'Say it, darling little witch. I want to hear you say it.'

'Say it?' she whispered slowly.

'That you want me.'

She shook her head. '*No!* I—I don't——'

'You're a liar,' he rasped. She detected a hint of amusement in the soft, deliberate tones. 'All that bit about promises doesn't mean a damned thing when it's like this. Just you and me, in bed, wanting each other. What the hell do promises mean then? Or anything else, for that matter?'

Her reply was lost as he caught the rosy tip of her breast between his lips and rotated it tormentingly with his tongue. The exquisite sensation was like no other she had ever felt and she cried out as she gripped his head, her fingers kneading frantically through his hair. His tongue traced a heated path lower to her navel where it paused, circling that erogenous zone. Meantime, the skilful hands were still continuing their exploration, leaving a trail of shivering delight across her belly, down her legs and up the sensitive skin of her inner thighs.

Her body was racked with long, deep shudders of pleasure that left her clinging to him, sobbing his name. His arms went around her, cradling her gently. 'Easy, Red, easy,' he soothed.

She gripped him convulsively, her fingers ploughing through the thick pelt on his chest, tracing with a sensation of wonder the taut outline of the masculine nipples.

He kissed her savagely. 'Now, do you want me?' he whispered fiercely.

'Yes, please, Simon,' she moaned. 'Please . . .'

This time, his kiss was long and drugging, leaving her a languid supplicant. 'That's good enough for me,' he whispered thickly.

Sliding his hands beneath her hips, he raised her for his invasion. With a sure instinct, his powerful body overwhelmed hers. She stiffened, the shock of pain rendering her helpless, making her writhe with agony against his chest. She could feel his surprise; her eyes, flaring open, saw the look of stunned amazement on his face, then he was lost in a turbulence of sensation over which he had no control. She clung instinctively to the broad, muscular back, her fingernails lacerating the flesh, her breath coming in hoarse, panting sobs. The pain was gradually absorbed in a pleasure that rose higher and higher until the peak became unbearable, then she exploded into a thousand small sensations, each aching with its own separate sweetness.

For long moments, she could do nothing but cling to the big, sweat-dampened body, as though it was an anchor. Then began the long, weightless slide downhill into a warm, languid bath of contentment. She sighed, her lids closing irresistibly.

She awakened slowly, gradually becoming aware of the heavy head cradled in her arms, the weight of the arm across her hip, and the slow rise and fall of his breathing. Her eyelids fluttered open. Her own breath quickened and she started to move when suddenly, warm fingers gripped her chin and her head was turned towards him. His lids were still heavy with the aftermath of sleep, but the eyes were keen and clear.

'Well, I'll be damned!' he said softly. 'The last thing I expected, Margaret, was a twenty-four-year-old virgin.'

Occasionally, in the beginning, he had called her Margaret. Abruptly, she was dragged back into the present, into a situation that began in Florida and seemed destined to end on a mountain top in Colorado. Her mind thought of and rejected half-a-dozen replies and finally came up with a bitter answer, 'Don't tell me you're having pangs of conscience?'

He paused, as though seriously considering her question.

'Nope,' he said cheerfully. 'Not a one. I'll admit I'm thinking an awful lot of things, but for the time being, I'll keep most of them to myself. Just satisfy my curiosity about one thing, if you will. How the hell did you keep brother-in-law Tony interested without losing your virginity?'

She stiffened. 'Suppose you tell me?' she demanded sarcastically. 'I'm sure you have an answer. You know everything.'

He smiled cynically. 'I figure you laid a smokescreen that fooled Barbara so she would give him up.' He shook his head in mock amazement. 'But I still don't understand it. You had Tony going around in circles. You aren't even his type, either. He was always extremely direct about garnering his pleasures. I would have said he was the last person in the world to be fooled by a professional tease.'

She raised her hand to strike him, but he caught it almost lazily.

'I misread your character altogether,' he went on thoughtfully. 'I assumed you were like all the other women who attracted Tony and I planned my revenge accordingly. Tony's type of women, I thought, would have found it hard as hell shacked up here in isolation, forced to do hard, slogging work. But you took it without a single yap of protest and even seemed to find it a challenge. I must admit I've been puzzled. It looks like I'm going to have to think again. There has to be some way to reach that cold little heart of yours.'

She stared at him fiercely. She felt dizzy with hatred. 'You'll never reach it, Simon Egan!' she said bitterly. 'If there's a cold heart in this house, it's yours, not mine! You should be jailed for abduction, rape——'

'Hardly rape, my dear. I distinctly heard you beg me to take you.' His smoky eyes narrowed on her flushed face. 'In fact, that might be the answer.' He raised himself on his elbow, his face hovering over hers. 'It's always better the second time,' he added softly, as his lips descended.

CHAPTER EIGHT

THE next time Meg awakened, it was morning. The room was empty, but the dented pillow beside her was enough to remind her of what had happened last night. She huddled beneath the blankets, shivering, remembering her abandoned responses to Simon. Last night, before falling asleep, they had made love again and Simon had made her reaffirm that she wanted him, her lips repeating a litany of desire until they were stopped by his mouth. Her cheeks reddened with embarrassment as she remembered how she had obeyed his hoarsely voiced commands like a slave to his bidding. They had made love in a savage burst of passion that had consumed her in its flames. And now, what? She dreaded having to meet Simon, face his knowing eyes, but finally, hunger drove her out of bed.

Neither of them, of course, had thought to bank the fire last night, but the stove had repaid past efforts by responding quickly, and there was a warm fire going. Simon had already made coffee and bacon was sizzling in the pan. He had apparently showered and dressed in his bedroom downstairs, and her eyes flickered away from the glimpse of his throat at the open neck of his flannel shirt. She caught a whiff of the spicy shaving lotion he used. Last night, it had been strong in her nostrils as she pressed kisses against that same throat, and in spite of herself, a series of strong erotic images rose to her mind, almost choking her.

'Want some breakfast?' he asked casually.

Thank heavens, he hadn't noticed anything! 'I'll get it myself if you'll move away from the stove. It's my job,' she added primly.

He ignored her. 'Sit down.' He proceeded to fill a coffee mug, which he passed to her, then filled a plate with bacon and eggs. He put it on the table, along with a second plate that had been warming on the back of the stove. He slid toast in the toaster, then sat down opposite her.

Neither of them said a word. Meg ate in stiff self-consciousness, but Simon seemed to her to be relaxed and perfectly at ease. In fact, the lines she had noticed yesterday morning were smoothed out today.

He finished first, then tilting his chair back on two legs, he eyed her with narrowed amusement.

'You're not going to sulk just because I made you admit you had an itch for me, are you?' When she didn't reply, he added provocatively, 'I thoroughly enjoyed myself last night.'

Meg almost choked. An *itch*! What a filthy, foul, common way to say it! Surely, as a writer, Simon could have thought of some other word to describe what was, at best, a horrible mistake on her part! She briefly contemplated rising and dumping the contents of the coffee pot over his head, but she knew he was taunting her to get a rise, and the best retaliation was to ignore his deliberately suggestive words.

A smile tugged at the corner of his mouth as he watched her. He had seen the flash of irritation that had deepened the green in her eyes and the visible effort she had made to restrain herself. He had even noticed the swift glance at the coffee pot and correctly guessed her reaction. Still speaking in a teasing voice, he asked, 'Where did you get the snowshoes?'

She looked at him sharply, instantly alerted. It would be no use lying—he meant to know the truth. 'In the attic.'

He grinned appreciatively. 'I overlooked the attic. Is there anything else up there I should know about?'

She glared at him haughtily. 'A pair of skis.'

'I suppose I can be thankful you didn't take off in those,' he drawled softly, meeting her eyes. There was a warning in them that she couldn't miss. It was promising retribution if she ever made the attempt. 'Want to learn how to use them?'

She blinked confusedly. 'Are you offering to teach me?'

'Uh, huh.'

She examined the idea cautiously, looking for flaws. 'Aren't you afraid I'll run away if I learn?' she demanded tartly.

'Nope. Learning a little should teach you just how little you really know.' He added aggravatingly. 'Besides, you aren't going anywhere. I'm going to make sure of that from now on.'

'Just how do you propose to do that?' she asked sarcastically.

'By keeping an eye on you. I'm moving my typewriter into the parlour so you can't sneak out while I'm busy. I've already turned up the heat so there won't be any need to chop wood. In fact, the wood stacked out there should do until we leave here. That way, when I go out, you go out, too. The rest of the time, I'm keeping the outside doors locked, just in case you're crazy enough to try something like this again.' He waited. 'Any more questions?'

She shrugged, stony-faced.

'Oh, yes, I forgot one thing.' His voice deepened with subtle amusement. 'From now on, we're sharing your bedroom.'

She burst into angry speech at that. 'Oh, no, we're not! You—you can't. I won't allow you to—besides—what has happened to your promise to make me suffer, wanting you?'

His grin widened. 'No point in punishing myself, too,' he said obliquely.

'I'll never forgive you! I'll hate you forever!'

'So you've told me, more than once. But before we leave here, you'll be singing a different tune.'

'What do you mean?'

'There is a fine line between love and hate. And now that I've learned how to stroke your fur, little cat, I think I can make you purr. Then, I'll really be revenged.

Meg felt as though her heart had been gripped in a vice of fear. 'You're c-c-crazy!' she stuttered. 'I-If you think, after all you've done—and said to me—I'll ever let you touch me again——'

'You'll be begging me, again, tonight.' His eyes were cold and glacial as they roamed her flushed, indignant face. 'Oh, yes, make no mistake. You can't stop me. And when I hear you beg for my love as you begged last night for my kisses, then maybe, just maybe, I'll feel the score is evened.'

She swallowed hard. 'You must think I'm a masochist.'

'No, but I'm a realist. I think I'm beginning to understand that cold little mind of yours. You lose it when that beautiful body takes over.' He smiled thinly. 'And, Red, that body is very responsive to me. Oh, yes, it is.'

She stood up abruptly and began to gather the dishes together with shaking hands. At the sink, with her back to him, she said shrilly, 'This discussion is pointless!'

'If you say so,' he agreed mockingly.

'I think you said something about teaching me to ski?' Now, more than ever, she had a need of learning how to get away!

'Ah, yes, the skiing lessons.' He paused thoughtfully. 'Are you still interested? I really wasn't sure,' he added softly.

Fat chance, Meg thought furiously. Now that the war between them had entered phase two, she was interested, all right!'

To her surprise, the skiing lesson was fun. Perhaps it was because Simon had dropped the mockery that was more hateful to her than his antagonism, and was treating her like he had in those first days in Florida. As though she was the kind of person he enjoyed being with. Or perhaps it was because she was outdoors. She hadn't done much of that since she got here. She found even the act of breathing exhilarating.

The lesson didn't last long. When Meg complained she was good for a longer one, Simon merely turned her around and pointed towards the house. 'We still have to get back.'

She was sobered immediately.

On the way back, he pointed out the deer tracks in the snow, and told her he saw them nearly every day he came out to chop wood. 'They're curious. And wary. Rather like you.' He grinned. 'They've had the mountain to themselves for so long they're naturally cautious about the humans in their midst. That's why my grandfather wanted this area left as it was. He was one of the first conservationists in this area, long before it was the popular thing to be. When my father brought up the idea of building a million dollar complex up here, with ski slopes, lodges, homes, the whole package deal, Gramps refused. That's why he and Gran left the mountain to me instead of my mother. Then, my father was furious!'

'Is that why you write under the name of Egan?'

'No, that was another quarrel—this time between my father and me. He refused to give me the year I needed to see if I could write. He thought writing was a foolish waste of time, and wanted me to go into the family business. A very domineering man, my father,' he added musingly.

'Really?' Meg asked drily. 'Rather like you, then?'

'Not at all,' he replied coolly. 'I would never impose my will on a child of mine. Anyway, my grandmother, who was living then, offered this place to me. She had the furnace put in and turned the house over to me for as long as I wanted to stay and see if I could write. I stayed up here one winter alone, doing my own cooking, and wrote my first novel. That was ten years ago, and it was the last time this house was occupied, for she died that spring.'

Ten years ago. That novel had been a big commercial success, a brilliant accomplishment for a young man of twenty-five. The movie that followed was a box office success, too. One still saw it on television.

During the days that followed, she and Simon maintained an uneasy truce. It was better than the cold, silent hatred of earlier days but it was not always friendly. He now typed in the parlour and kept his door locked, except when he used the short wave radio. Since the 'phone lines to Brennan's Pass seemed to be permanently down, he checked in every day. Meg saw where he kept it—in the closet—but she never was given an opportunity to get near it, or the 'phone. She would have liked to call Chris and thank him for his kindness, although she no longer had the same desperate desire to leave Simon.

Although there were moments when their hostility flared into angry words, there were other times when they were in accord. The idea of the quilt amused him and he told her things about his grandmother's life which she could incorporate into it.

However, the façade of normality they kept up during the day was torn down each night, as their bed became a battlefield. Simon employed a highly practised form of seduction to break down her barriers. Sometimes, it did not take long—a kiss, a touch—and she would be clinging to him, her body taut with desire. But he was not satisfied with just that. He wanted more—her subjugation—to make her reach the depths of humiliation—before he would take her with that driving intensity that enslaved her senses. Over and over again, she must reaffirm her craving, his mastery over her.

'Please, Simon, don't make me say it——' she would beg.

He would brush his mouth across the outline of her lips. 'But I want yoy to, Red.'

'I—want—you. I want you to make love to me.' She avoided looking into the smoky eyes that seemed to be searching into the depths of her soul.

'Again.' He raised his head from her throat, where his tongue had been teasing the shuddering little pulse there.

'Please, Simon, don't——'

'*Yes!* I want to hear it. For the first time in your cheating little life, you're feeling an honest emotion. Or as near to it as you're capable.' His lips twisted. 'Good, old-fashioned lust. You want me as badly as I want you.'

'It isn't lust,' she whispered painfully. 'I don't know what it is, but it isn't lust.'

'It surely isn't love,' he retorted, the contemptuous mockery making her feel cheap and shoddy and smudging the memory of the love she once had for him.

'All right, so it's lust!' She almost shrieked the words at him. 'Is that what you want to hear?'

She tried to twist away, but he captured her easily, his roving hand arousing her until she was gasping and moaning under his body. He took her then, in a wild tangle of arms and legs, as though he needed to prove something to himself as well as to her.

As Christmas approached, it snowed again, a gentle soft snow that batted at the window panes with baby fingers. The old house seemed to sigh and settle down for its winter's sleep. With the curtains drawn, and a fire on the hearth, Meg's bedroom was a cosy haven of warmth. Simon had apparently decided to take a holiday from writing, so they read companionably or listened to the radio while Meg quilted. When they got hungry, one of them would go downstairs for food and bring it up to the room on a tray. Most of the time, Meg wore the top to his pyjamas, and he wore the bottoms, or they wore nothing at all. They made love sweetly, tenderly, and Meg was happier than she had ever been in her life.

Meg knew that she was in love with Simon again, or probably, her love had never really been killed. At times, she was perilously close to forgetting why she was there, and that nothing had changed. His vengeance would be complete if he could bring her to gasp out words of love in his arms. Knowing this, she locked her lips and let her body speak for her. Hadn't he once said he found it responsive to his?

The next day, it was Christmas Eve. The radio had been playing carols all day, but Simon was apparently unaware of the date until she mentioned it. They were getting ready to go outside to inspect the bird feeders.

'You're right,' he said, consulting his calendar. 'Would you like a tree?'

'A tree? A Christmas tree?'

'Why not?' He grinned. It's customary.'

The wind was harsh that day and Simon's ski mask was crusted with ice by the time he finished cutting and hauling home the little tree. Meg pulled a turkey out of the freezer and baked a pumpkin pie, and that night, they trimmed the tree with strips of aluminium foil and strings of popcorn. Simon stayed at his typewriter after she went to bed, and the next morning, he surprised her by presenting her with a quilt stand he had made.

She was confused by the degree of pleasure she derived from the simple gift. Simon seemed amused by her compliments and exclamations of delight.

'I hammered it together when I made the Christmas tree stand, and last night, I sandpapered and varnished it. I remember my grandmother hanging her quilts on something like this.

Nothing was said about the gift Meg had once shyly offered him with her love, only to have it spurned, but she wondered if it had been that memory that prompted Simon to make the stand.

In late January, it got much colder. The temperature dipped, and Simon kept fires in both the parlour and Meg's bedroom. He was working hard to finish the book and although he never talked about it, Meg knew he must be nearing the end. She was dreading it, for she had a feeling the end of the book would see a change in their relationship. She had more than half the squares of her quilt finished, too, and kept them draped across her stand. Going by what Simon had told her about his grandmother, Meg had used her talent for drawing to design a simple picture for each square. Only one square was different, the one devoted to her own childhood.

After about a week, the weather warmed slightly, enough for them to go outside and check on the bird feeders. Simon had planted the Christmas tree outside in the snow and kept it hung with suet balls. It had been picked clean, and Meg found a marmot in one of the bird feeders, stealing food. His furry little tail twitched indignantly as he saw her, and her laughter rang out unexpectedly, bringing Simon's head sharply around.

When they got back into the house, he took her hand and led her into the parlour. With the red plush curtains Meg had hung and the hearth rug Simon had brought down from the attic, it was a different room from the one in which he had cruelly rejected her on their wedding night. Meg was not even thinking of that when he gently removed her clothing, once piece at a time, his eyes gleaming smokily in the firelight. His lips made contact with hers, feathering their outline with a series of light, delicate kisses, then moving on to her eyelids and forehead. His hands softly stroked her face, following the trail of his kisses, then he drew back and stared at her. Her hair was spilling over her shoulders, glowing like burnished fire, and her green eyes stared back with the slumbering quality of a cat's eyes.

'Undress me,' he commanded hoarsely.

She removed his clothes shyly, with trembling hands, her eyelids sweeping her flushed cheeks.

'You're a spellbinder, green-eyed witch. Do you know that? Tell me, my sweet, do you have any idea of the effect you have on me?' He groaned and pulled her down to the rug, where his lips captured hers in a long, deep kiss.

She was quivering with delight at his words. For the first time, she initiated the caresses, forgetting her shyness, her fear, as she kissed him hungrily on the mouth, the throat and eyes, her hands twisting restlessly in the springing curls on his chest, while she mouthed small, cooing endearments. Finally, he pulled her to him roughly and brought them both to a shuddering peak of pleasure that left them drained and languid. She looked up to see him smiling at her tenderly and involuntarily, spontaneously, the words rose to her lips. 'I love you, Simon.' She could no more have dammed them back than she could have halted the flow of the seasons, but as soon as she uttered them, she knew she had made a mistake.

He did not respond or show her that he even heard her. Instead, he rose and pulling a blanket off the davenport, wrapped them both in it so they could lie before the fire. She was unbelievably tired and almost at once, fell asleep in his arms. When she awakened, she was alone. She heard Simon's voice from behind the closed bedroom door, and she knew he was calling in to the ranger station, which he did once a day. She remembered what she had said and knew she had been a fool. Now, what had been beautiful and special seemed wanton and cheap, and she sat up hastily and began to pull on her clothes. She was glad that she had dressed when Simon came out of the bedroom, fully dressed, and started to work without even looking her way.

Later, she wondered why she had said it. Although it was true, it would have been a simple matter to keep quiet about it—that is, if she wanted to continue to live with him, and she knew now that she did. He had said that once he had her love, the score would be even. Yet, knowing this, she had spoken, merely because she had wanted to give him something freely, from the heart.

She was not such a fool as to expect an answer in kind but neither did she expect an immediate withdrawal, and that was what happened. He spent the rest of the day at his typewriter, barely speaking during meals, the old easy friendship gone, blown away as though on the wind. What she was left with was nothing but a chilly courtesy and blank indifference.

He was still at his typewriter when Meg went upstairs, and when he still had not come to bed at dawn, she knew it was over, he had evened the score. Meg was not a fool, in spite of her foolishness, and she knew she had given him an easy victory. Those wretched admissions of lust, wrung from her in the heat of passion, had not been what he wanted at all. He had wanted to hurt her, and now that he had, he no longer wanted her.

Yet, in spite of his victory, Meg felt that she had won one of her own. Before, she had been like a person with a terrible, festering wound. Now, the abcess had been opened and drained. Hate had twisted her, making her harsh and cruel, eating at her from inside. Now, she was healed. She didn't regret her love for Simon. She was a better person for it. And if she could be granted a boon, she would wish that Simon, too, had found a sort of peace.

The next two days he spent at his typewriter like a

man demented, driving himself to finish the novel. Meg knew that when he did, he would be ready to leave the mountain, and would be taking her with him for that divorce.

The third morning, she awakened to the sound of a snowmobile. She leaped from her bed just as the engine whined to a throttling stop beneath her window, which was above the porch. Looking out, she saw it was pulled up close under the eaves, and she could not see the driver. With frantic haste, she pulled on her robe and slipped her feet into furry slippers. She raced downstairs, stumbling over her robe in her hurry to reach the front door. It was locked. Running to the window that looked out on to the porch, she saw a line of footprints leading across the snowy floor to Simon, who stood with his back to her as he talked to the two people in the snowmobile. He was handing a brown-wrapped package to the driver, and she knew it must be his manuscript. At the edge of the porch, a slim, expensive piece of woman's luggage rested. Meg's eyes sharpened on the passenger in the snowmobile. Simon was lifting her out and Meg could see it was a woman by her matching make-up case and the way she clung to his neck. She rapped sharply and tugged frantically at the window catch but all she accomplished was a sharp command from Simon to the driver that sent him off in a burst of speed.

Simon deposited the woman on the porch and she stripped off the ski mask and her cap, laughing as she tossed back her mane of red-gold hair. It was Carol.

CHAPTER NINE

NATURALLY, she looked exquisite. When she came in laughing, after Simon unlocked the door, she glowed like a girl in a Swiss travel poster, with snow lightly powdering her shoulders and the bloom of good health reddening her cheeks and lips. When she saw Meg, she gave a glad little cry of joy and rushed at her, throwing her arms around her.

'Oh, Meg, darling, how wonderful to see you again! I've been so lonely for you—so blue! I thought I'd never see you again!' She drew back, blinking away tears and uttering a shamed little laugh as she looked at Simon. 'Look at me! Breaking down like a silly little fool! B-But I can't help it!' She turned back to her stepsister. 'Oh, Meg, isn't this snow gorgeous? I've been throwing snowballs and tramping through it like a kid ever since I got to Colorado! It's so white and beautiful—and it makes you feel so *good*!'

She was real. She looked like Carol, and she certainly acted and talked like Carol—or at least the way Carol did on those rare occasions in Meg's presence when she wanted to impress someone. Meg dimly sensed she wanted to impress Simon, and her eyes moved slowly towards him. He was watching Carol with an indulgent little smile, and Meg felt sick.

'What are you doing here?' she asked flatly.

'Why, Simon sent for me, of course.' Carol turned a helpless face to Simon, as though asking him to explain to Meg. She had been taking off her ski suit—again with Simon's help—and Meg saw that beneath it, she wore a powder blue velour jumpsuit, trimly belted at the waist and clinging closely to her braless breasts. She tossed her hair back with a practised swing, and Meg saw that it had been given a professional cut. She was wearing a new brand of lipstick, too—one that didn't war with her hair—and she had learned how to use eye make-up discreetly. She looked and smelled expensive.

'Simon's Mr Selby found me in Miami. I hope you don't mind me calling you Simon,' she broke off to ask appealingly, 'but your friend Sam talked so much about you that I feel I know you already.'

'Sam?' Meg asked.

'Sam McKay, my lawyer,' Simon explained briefly, in a clipped voice. 'You've never met him—he couldn't make our wedding.' He was still watching Carol.

'He brought me up the mountain in that adorable little car.' She was talking to Meg but looking at Simon. With a muttered excuse, Meg turned towards the stairs. Simon stopped her before she had taken a step.

'How about putting some sheets on the other bed for Carol?' he asked coolly.

'Oh, no, I'll do it myself!' Carol chirped, picking up her make-up case and starting towards the stairs. 'I don't intend to have anyone doing *my* work. Sam told me how you were roughing it up here, chopping wood and building fires and I—I just think it sounds wonderful! I'm dying to get out in that snow and do my part. I may not know much about chopping wood, Simon, but Meg can tell you I'm not afraid of housework! The least I can do is put the sheets on my own bed.'

Meg turned without a word and led the way upstairs, with Simon following Carol and carrying her suitcase. She went straight to the linen closet and brought out a set of sheets and pillow cases. There were plenty of blankets on the top shelf, but they were out of her reach. Carrying the sheets into the other bedroom, which looked cold and bare without curtains or a rug,

Meg dumped them on the bed, then stalked out without a word.

Why had he brought Carol here? Was this to be phase three in her punishment? Suddenly, all the ugliness of their betrayal hit her in the stomach, and she doubled over, clutching the bedpost for support, as wave after wave of sickness hit her. With a supreme effort, she forced herself to stay calm by erasing all thoughts of Carol from her mind. She could do it, she told herself grimly. Last night, she had turned a defeat into a victory by thinking beautiful thoughts. Now, she must ignore Carol and yes, even Simon, and all the probabilities of what Carol's return into her life meant by making her mind a deliberate blank. She hung on to the bedpost as beads of sweat popped out on her brow, but slowly, her heaving stomach righted itself. She straightened and looked at herself in the mirror. She felt better but her face was still white. She looked awful, of course, but she did not bother with lipstick or make-up. She seldom did, and she was not going to start now and give Simon the idea that she was trying to compete with Carol's exquisite beauty.

She was brushing and braiding her tawny hair into a single braid when there was a soft knock at the door. It was Carol. She entered apologetically, her eyes anxiously watching Meg.

'Look, Meg,' she began hurriedly. 'I know you're mad about something, but——'

'I don't think you're qualified to judge how I feel, Carol,' Meg replied levelly. 'But I'll ask you again. How does it happen you're here?'

'You mean you don't know *anything* about it?' Carol sounded genuinely perplexed.

'Do you really think I would want to see you again, under the circumstances?' Meg asked drily.

Carol flushed. 'Well, no,' she began defensively. 'But what was I to think when that man—that Mr Selby—

found me? He said you were married and your husband had hired him to find me. Well, naturally, I assumed you'd begun to worry about me, and then, when I got to Denver, and Sam met Mr Selby and me at the airport, and bought me all those wonderful clothes, I—— —— And, then, he told me who you had married. At first, I didn't know who Simon Egan was, because you know, I don't read much,' she added ingenuously, 'but as soon as Sam told me the names of his movies, I thought dear sweet Meg has done this for me, so I can get my break!' Her false eyelashes fluttered but she must have caught a glimpse of Meg's expression, because she added with a hint of panic. 'No one even *hinted* that the whole thing wasn't your idea! And it wasn't until I got here and saw your face that I realised you didn't know a thing about it!'

'All right, so you thought it was my idea.' Meg put down her brush and looked at her wearily. 'Now you know it wasn't. It was my husband's. But I don't want you here, Carol, so I expect you to clear out. You can start by telling Simon——'

'Meg, I can't,' Carol gasped. 'I was really down and out when that Mr Selby found me. I had left Kit—well, he really kicked me out. He claimed I was cheating on him and——'

'Were you?'

Carol looked blank and didn't bother to answer. 'Oh, Meg, I hoped you wouldn't be so—so *bitter*! Why can't you put what happened behind you, and realise I was just a panicky kid who'd got in over her head and had nowhere to turn? After all, we *are* sisters! And now, you've fallen on your feet, just as I knew you would if I just walked out and let you go it on your own. Remember? I told you that you didn't need me messing up your life, being a drain on you while you supported me! Once you were on your own, without me to worry about, you found a husband and—— Why, you really owe it all to me!' she added earnestly. 'Afterwards, I looked *everywhere* for you, to ask you to forgive me for messing up your life. I was just about on the streets when that man found me——'

'You don't look like you've been suffering,' Meg said coldly.

'That's because I went to a first-class beauty salon in Denver!' Carol's chin wobbled reproachfully. 'Every stitch I have in the world is on my back or in that suitcase, and it was bought with your husband's money! Sam opened an account for me and ... I didn't bring a thing with me when Mr Selby told me where I'd be going. Well, as a matter of fact, Kit sold everything I had to get money for—for *drugs*, Meg! I was so shocked! Oh, I've been in such a lot of trouble. You *can't* think about kicking me out!'

Meg looked at her tiredly, her mind automatically sifting and rejecting half of Carol's babble. If Kit was into drugs, Carol had known all about it. Undoubtedly, too, she had cheated on Kit, but apparently, she had had a rough time. However, when she went looking for Meg, it was not to ask for forgiveness but money—and right now, she was thinking that she, not Meg, had fallen on her feet. Anyway, Meg's threats were so much bluster because Carol had no intention of leaving, unless she was thrown out by Simon. And she would soon learn that he would never do that so long as she played her role of the beaten, submissive little sister so well. No, she would wrap herself around Simon like a warm, cloying little kitten and cling and cling and cling, with those sharp, needle-point little nails of hers. In a way, he deserved what he was going to get, Meg thought sardonically. He hadn't believed her truths— let's see how long he swallows Carol's lies.

'All right, Carol, you win. You can stay.'

'Thank you, darling. Although, really, it was up to Simon to decide when I should leave. He brought me here,' she reminded Meg delicately. It was a small, subtle gauntlet, just large enough for a kitten's paw, but it was a challenge, nevertheless. Carol was entering the ranks of competing with Meg for her husband's attention.

Carol turned away and Meg saw that she had exchanged her boots for a pair of gold heelless sandals with two-inch spike heels. 'Carol. I hope you meant what you said.' Carol turned back, puzzled. 'About that division of labour? I'm going to take you up on it.'

'Well, naturally, Meg.' Carol tossed her head indignantly.

Naturally. Meg smiled grimly, remembering all of Carol's cover-up words and phrases. 'Naturally' was one of them she used often and was supposed to express hurt at not being trusted. Naturally, one cooked and cleaned in high-heel sandals and powder blue velour. Naturally, one had no intention of taking advantage of one's sister—not to mention one's sister's husband. Well, Carol might find herself up against the original immovable object when it came to Simon. He would expect her to work and it should be interesting to see who won. Carol had never made a bed or washed a dish in her life, and she was the world's worse cook. And if there was one thing Meg had learned about Simon, it was that he appreciated good cooking. Wait until he sampled Carol's, for she, Meg, was not going to do anything more than *her* share of the cleaning and cooking.

In the bathroom, she saw that Carol had already spread out. Her make-up, hot curler set and combs and brushes littered the sink counter, and a lipstick-stained towel had been flung on the tank top. Give her another day or two, when her discarded clothing and wet towels were all over the floor, and she would hear Simon's roar of disapproval, unless Meg gave in and cleaned it first. That was usually what happened whenever she tried to teach Carol good housekeeping methods. But not this time. Meg smiled softly as she listened to Carol swishing coat hangers as she unpacked in her bedroom.

Downstairs, Simon was at the kitchen table, hunched over a cup of coffee.

'Do you want breakfast?' Meg asked.

'It's a little late for that, isn't it?' he snapped. He added moodily, 'You are a mean-minded little bitch, aren't you? Couldn't you have extended a warmer welcome to your house guest? Oh, I know, I know,' he added, as Meg opened her mouth. 'She's not your sister, merely your stepsister. Are you the *ugly* stepsister, Meg? Like the one in the fairy tale,' he added cruelly.

Meg flinched, then walked steadily into the pantry where she took a roast from the freezer. When she returned, she dropped it into the sink with a solid clunk and reached for the tap with trembling hands. She felt like she had been slapped, and she was having a hard time clinging to her policy of indifference.

'I don't want her here,' she said stonily.

Simon flung up his head. He looked angry and disgusted. 'That's very obvious, I must say, but you're damned well going to have her here!' he snapped. 'Do you know where Selby found her, or do you even care? She was on the streets of Miami, peddling her body! A girl like that!'

'Yes, she told me Kit threw her out.'

'Is that all you can say?' he demanded harshly. 'Is that the best you can do, when you're responsible for the mess that youngster got into?'

Meg stared at the roast dully. It had been a mistake to get it out. It was frozen solid and it was going to take a low, slow oven to thaw it out and cook it. Someone would have to watch Stove and she knew she was incapable of doing it; at least, she was today. Simon wouldn't want to, and of course, Carol wouldn't know how. She picked up the roast and carried it back to the freezer. Simon watched her in irritable silence.

'You *did* hear what I was saying, didn't you?' he asked ironically. 'Did you know that man she was living with had a drug record?'

Meg shrugged. 'She wanted to go with him.'

'That may be true. In fact, I guess it is, since you wouldn't lie about something that is so easily proved. But you made it impossible for her to stay. Carol felt she had to get out after learning about Barbara and what you'd done to her!' Meg turned and stared at him blankly. 'Oh, I talked to Selby, and Sam, too, on the short wave. Sam was waiting the other night when I checked in with the ranger station, he and Selby both. Carol had unburdened herself to both of them—told them you'd done something so awful she couldn't stick around.' He glared at her violently. 'Well, what about it? Have you got anything to say for yourself?'

Meg's numbness abruptly left her. Her stomach heaved and she threw Simon a white, panicky look before clamping her hands over her mouth and racing towards the stairs.

She made it to the bathroom, just in time. When she recovered enough to realise what was going on about her, she saw that Simon was standing nearby, a frown on his face, handing her a wet cloth, and Carol was hovering beyond him in the doorway.

'What's wrong with you?' he asked brusquely.

'I don't know. I must be getting a virus,' she mumbled weakly. 'Go away.'

'Nonsense. You need to be in bed and you don't need to be alone right now. Carol——'

'*No!* I do want to be alone and I don't need anyone's help to get to bed!' she said sullenly. She sat on the side of the tub and wiped her face with the wet cloth.

'All right,' he said mildly. 'Go to bed, then.'

When he came in five minutes later, she was lying in

bed with her face turned towards the wall. 'Go away,' she muttered.

For answer, he popped a thermometer in her mouth and put a cup of tea on her bedside table.

'You need to drink this if you can. You haven't had a thing since last night, and you're going to become dehydrated if you don't get some liquids in your stomach,' he said crisply. He removed the thermometer and looked at it. 'Hmm. Normal. What is wrong, Meg? Are you pregnant?'

She raised herself and stared at him, thunderstruck. '*No!* Of course not!' she gasped in a horrified whisper. '*No!* Absolutely not! Oh, God, I hope not!'

'The possibility had occurred to me,' he said drily, 'And if you are, the sooner we know, the better. Surely you can see that?' Something about her palsied look of sheer horror got to him, for he added irritably, 'All right, you've just picked up a virus! You'd better stay in bed for the rest of the day. Here, let me help you get comfortable.'

He reached out to pull at her sweater just as she raised her hands to pull it off. Their hands collided and as though the contact had triggered off all of Meg's hostility, she began striking at him blindly, hitting him wherever she could.

'No! *No!* Let me go! Don't touch me! I don't want your help—never again! Don't touch me, I tell you!' she cried hysterically.

He gripped her hands and held them firmly, his face dark with anger. 'All right, you little wildcat, I'm not going to touch you. If you weren't ill, I'd teach you some manners, but in case you're cooking up a fever, and have some crack-brained notion in your head, I assure you I haven't the slightest desire to touch you, in any way, if that's what you're worried about! And lower your voice. We are supposed to be on our honeymoon. You don't want your sister to think we're already getting a divorce, do you?'

'Why not?' She flung the words at him recklessly, out of her pain. 'It would be the truth, wouldn't it? Don't tell me you're going back on your promise? And after the convincing performance I put on, too,' she added savagely.

There was a silence. Then he gripped her chin and turned her face roughly up to his. 'Are you trying to tell me you lied to me the other day?'

'At the risk of putting a sizeable dent in your ego, I'm afraid I'm going to have to admit I did.' She was filled with a heady sense of power and wanted to hurt him— to get a little of her own back. She added mockingly, 'I realise I'm ruining my chance of getting that divorce as early as I would like, but not even for that pleasure can I continue to put up with your pawing me at night. It makes me sick.'

He smiled slowly. 'Now I know you're lying,' he said softly. 'Which means you are lying about it all. Why?'

'How do you know I'm lying?' she cried passionately. 'It's merely your own conceit that makes you refuse to admit it!'

His fingers slowly traced a delicate line across her face before he released her chin. 'But I do know, Red. I know all about you. I can see through you all the way. You're about as transparent as glass.'

She stared at him in baffled frustration, thinking of all the many times she had told him the truth, only to have it disbelieved. And now, when it was most important he should think she had been lying, he persisted in believing she had told the truth.

'But didn't you claim it would take an actress to fool Tony and Barbara?' she demanded fiercely. 'And I did it! Face it, Simon! You can't have it both ways. I can't be so transparent with you and yet, acted my head off with them. Or,' she added with sweet viciousness, 'is it that you want to believe me because you're following in Tony's footsteps? Are you beginning to run in circles just as he did, and crave his woman, Simon?'

His face darkened and the smile on his lips froze into a thin, cruel line. 'Put that out of your mind, my dear,' he said evenly. 'I don't crave the woman Tony wanted. And you, despite your boast, don't have me running in circles, wondering where I am.' A thread of amusement laced his voice. 'I know exactly where I am with you, Meg, and you are incapable of being all things to all men.' He leaned over and pulled up the blanket to her chin. 'Now, have your day in bed and enjoy it,' he added calmly.

As the door closed gently behind it, Meg thought dully that he had certainly made it clear, in case she hadn't already got the message. He didn't crave her. Which was too bad, for she was beginning to desperately crave him.

CHAPTER TEN

MEG did have her day in bed, too exhausted after her emotional orgy to do anything else. She knew she had been mad to fight with Simon. She could never win, and how easily, with a few well-chosen words, he had punished her for what she had said. She didn't know why she had started it, unless it was because she had been thrown off balance by his suggestion that she might be pregnant.

The idea was absurd, of course. She couldn't be pregnant. Her mind played idly with dates, then she fumbled on the bedside table with the calendar. She grew increasingly frantic as she flipped pages, checked days, then subsided against the pillows. She *was* pregnant! How could she bear it? Pregnant—and forced to live with a resentful Simon. For that's what it would mean, at least until the baby had a legal name. She knew Simon well enough to know he wouldn't shirk his duty there. And after that, yoked to him by an unwanted baby, squabbling over custody rights, money, all the sordid details of a messy divorce! She couldn't think of any greater punishment. Thank God, she had repudiated the suggestion so forcefully! He had believed her, and he might continue to believe her if she could get away before he knew.

Frowning, her mind sifted painfully through their conversation, something niggling at it. What had he said? 'If there's a chance you are, the sooner we know, the better.' What had he meant exactly? An *abortion*? Meg stilled as the certainty grew. She had never really given the right-to-life law much thought for she firmly believed a woman should have the right to say what was done with her own body, and there were plenty of times when an abortion was a medical necessity. But to abort her baby—*Simon*'s baby—merely because it was an inconvenience, seemed to her to be an obscenity. She doubled over, wrapping her arms protectively about herself. Never! She wouldn't do it or allow it to be done to her. But Simon must never know.

Meg looked around the room apathetically. It looked dusty and unkempt. She didn't feel like doing anything about it, although she was going to have to try. She couldn't let Simon guess she was still feeling ill.

She rose determinedly, pleased to find that her nausea had disappeared. When Carol popped her head in a short time later, Meg was tidying up her room.

'You're better, I see?'

There was a note of disappointment in her voice, which was the last thing Meg had expected. She looked at her curiously.

'Some, but I'm taking it easy for a while. You and Simon are going to have to carry on without me.'

That suited Carol. A look of relief spread over her face and she said eagerly, 'I don't think you should rush things. Just stay in your room and take it easy. I don't mind bringing up your trays. We've been playing gin rummy in the kitchen, and he's been telling me about Hollywood.' Then, in case Meg might be tempted to interfere, she added hastily, 'I don't think you're well enough to be around people yet. You may have something catching.'

The mystery was now explained. Carol was in the kitchen trying out her kittenish wiles on Simon. And what about him? The last thing she would have expected of him was that he would enjoy a whole day of Carol's uninterrupted company. She would have thought an hour would have bored him to the point of rudeness, but apparently not. Men were strange—and of course, Carol *was* beautiful.

'Don't worry,' Meg assured her drily. 'I haven't any desire to crash in on your party.'

She spent the rest of the day in her room. Since learning about the baby, a sort of numbness had blanked out her feelings. She no longer cared that Simon had brought Carol here to punish her, then fallen hook, line and sinker for her lies. He was welcome to her—they deserved one another.

When Carol looked in on her just before dinner, she found Meg rocking in the firelight, her eyes dreamily vacant. Carol looked at her sharply. 'I don't believe you're sick at all!'

Meg smiled at her tranquilly. 'I feel fine.'

Carol was taken aback. 'Does that mean you're joining us for dinner?'

'Yes, I'm hungry.'

Carol looked so upset that Meg knew she had put a damper on her plans for the evening. Apparently, the gin rummy game had paid off, Meg thought humorously. She was surprised at her own lack of jealousy. The only emotion she felt, if one could call it emotion, was enjoyment at Carol's transparency. Obviously, she thought Meg's presence would throw a spanner into her flirtation with Simon. Meg felt like assuring her it wouldn't stop Simon at all.

'Are you going to wear those old things?'

Meg looked at her sweater and jeans, then at Carol, realising for the first time how she was dressed. She was wearing a beautiful dress of emerald green silk, but at one time, she would have been asking for a case of pneumonia to wear it in this house. Made with a series of flounces on the skirt, one shoulder was bare and the other was held up by a big silk bow. It was ridiculously inappropriate for a meal in the kitchen of a cold, draughty house.

'Yes,' Meg said mildly.

'Honestly, you kill me, Meg! Simon said you were in

Denver for four days before the wedding, buying winter clothes, and with all his money, *that* is the best you can come up with!' Carol eyed the practical jeans and sweater disgustedly. 'You know, don't you, that you're just asking for it if someone steals your husband? You just don't deserve to have him!'

Meg shrugged. 'At least I won't be the one with the goose pimples.'

Carol flushed angrily. 'You deserve whatever you get!' she warned her, then flounced out.

The table was set for three when Meg came into the kitchen. Simon was standing by the stove, his face reddened by the heat, testing a pot of chilli. He was dressed about as usual, in black jeans and a black polo neck sweater, but he had apparently been paying Carol a teasing compliment on her dress, for she was laughing and flipping the bow with her finger.

He looked up, his eyes intent, as Meg entered. 'Are you feeling better?'

'I don't know,' she said calmly. 'I'm going to wait and see.'

Carol insisted that Meg sit down, then fussed about, making a big thing of putting out napkins, silverware and filling the water glasses. She might have been the hostess and Meg a polite guest. Meg felt as though she *was* a guest—no, an observer, on a little island of immunity, watching the three of them from afar. She was tranquil as she ate her chilli. Simon kept casting small worried glances at her as though she puzzled him. He's probably worried sick that I'm pregnant, Meg thought tolerantly, because he'd hate to have an abortion on his conscience.

Carol was feeling injured. She had had Simon to herself for the whole day, and her flirtation with him had reached a delicate stage. She had already come to the conclusion that he was too good to be wasted on Meg. Marriage hadn't improved her pious goody-goody outlook, and Carol felt justified in taking Simon away from her. After all, just *anybody* would do for Meg, whereas Simon was special. And Simon liked her. He'd been alternately teasing and flirting with her all day and there had been a certain look in his eye. Meg had no right to spoil things!

Carol felt peeved, but at least, Simon was picking up his cue. He had opened a bottle of wine, and her glass never seemed to be empty. Miss Goody Two-shoes over there, who had abstained, was watching her detachedly, and something about her expression drove Carol to recklessness. She intended *proving* to Meg that Simon was no longer interested in her! Carol, who had no head for alcohol, was fast getting drunk.

Meg listened without interest as Simon led Carol to talk about her childhood, drawing her out with adroit questions. As usual, Carol presented herself as the misunderstood and unappreciated younger sister, forced, because of Meg's jealousy, to always have to accept second-best.

'I would have been much better off if Meg had let me be adopted when Mom died. I was only eleven and could have lived with someone who really could take care of me. Someone who could afford a child like me.'

'Let's see, Meg was about seventeen then, wasn't she?'

'Yes, and much too young to take care of a sensitive child like me!' Carol's voice rose querulously. 'When the social worker interviewed her in the hospital, Meg lied and said I was her sister. Her real sister. Naturally, it all seemed legal, and no one took me away from her.'

'Didn't anyone ever ask you how you felt about it?'

'We-e-el, I told Mrs McNeely. She was our neighbour who took care of me while Meg was sick. She got mad and told me I wasn't to hurt Meg by telling her I didn't want to stay with her. Of course, she thought Meg was wonderful and was always yapping about how grateful

I should be. *Grateful!* Because I had to live in a cheap place, and do without things I wanted, and all because Meg made that stupid promise to Mom!'

'Perhaps she thought you might be put into a foster home?' Simon suggested idly.

'Oh, but I wouldn't have!' Carol said quickly. 'I was told by lots of people that I was a natural for adoption by someone rich. Because I was so pretty, you see. Sometimes I wondered if that wasn't why Meg did it, because she wanted to spoil my life!'

Meg had heard all that before, too, and it never ceased to amaze her that Carol was so childish as to continue to believe in those mythical rich parents. As she grew older, the story grew, too, until Carol finally believed it had all been a plot on Meg's part. Surely Simon knew better, although he had been raptly listening to the whole story.

Apparently, Carol sensed a trace of scepticism in the air, too, in spite of her wine-fogged brain, for she laughed a little uneasily. 'Of course, I can't really blame poor Meg,' she said hurriedly. 'The poor darling wasn't really herself in the hospital. She cracked up, you know.'

'No, I didn't know,' Simon said deeply. 'How do you mean cracked up?'

'She had a nervous breakdown.' Carol raised her suddenly full glass and drank, then glanced at Meg's blank face. Gathering assurance from Simon's interest, she went on, 'She wasn't hurt in the accident—just bruised and shaken—but she was driving and Mom was killed—and I guess she felt it was partly her fault it happened. At least, she always blamed herself.' Carol paused delicately, her innocent eyes gazing earnestly at Simon. '*I* didn't blame her, but Meg felt she had made me an orphan. She wouldn't even ride in a car for ages, and she hasn't driven one to this day!'

'Indeed?'

His voice sounded odd, and Carol glanced at him quickly. He wasn't looking at her, but at Meg, who was staring with a remote expression at the sink full of dirty dishes. Carol, who felt rather defensive about those dishes, felt a flash of irritation. Was Meg *hinting*?

As a matter of fact, Meg had learned a new trick. She was tuning Carol out, and that way, she was not even hearing all those familiar accusations that used to hurt her so much. And Simon, too. She was blanking his face and voice right out of her mind. When she looked at him, all she saw was a blur without a face. His eyes—those wonderful eyes that could darken equally with passion or anger, or become as clear and cool as a summer storm—did not even exist for her any longer. And his mouth? Where was it? Suddenly, she saw it, and there was something about the hard shape that made her know he was angry. If he was angry, it was with her, because he had been feeding Carol wine and flattery all evening.

She stood up and said politely, 'I think I will go back to my room, if you will excuse me.'

She heard Simon's voice calling to her but she kept right on walking up the stairs.

CHAPTER ELEVEN

CAROL followed her within a couple of minutes. Meg heard her heels on the stairs, and considered briefly shutting her door so that she wouldn't have to talk to her but Carol went straight to her room. Ten minutes later, she came out and paused in the doorway of Meg's room, where she sat reading.

'Simon told me to come up and change so I could do the dishes,' she commented softly. 'But I think he really wants to be alone with me. Do you think he'll like this?'

Meg looked up. Apparently, these days, Carol had given up wearing bras, and the deeply plunging neckline of her caftan showed a generous portion of her bare breasts. It was made of ice blue velvet and was so much like the one Meg had worn her wedding night that for a brief moment, her armour was pierced and she flinched with pain. Carol saw from Meg's expression that she had got through her guard and she moved inside the room, closing the door.

'Am I right, Meg? Is your marriage on the rocks?' she asked, smug with satisfaction. 'What happened? Did all this togetherness get Simon down? I know he's not the type to want a dull work horse like you. Of course, he would want a cook and bed partner while he was up here for the winter, but what beats me is why he *married* you!'

Meg laughed mockingly. 'You're slipping Carol, not to have guessed. That's the cream of the jest—his reason for marrying me.'

Carol hesitated, puzzled. 'I guess he thought he was attracted to you . . .' she began uncertainly.

'Oh, no,' Meg said pleasantly. Oh, I thought he was

in love with me, but I was wrong. He didn't want a cook or a bed partner either: for that, he wouldn't have had to marry me. He could have found plenty of those who were girls like you, Carol, much prettier and livelier than me. Not plain, ordinary, stupid girls like me.'

Carol frowned. 'What are you trying to say? That he thought you had money—or was knocked over by your brains—or sorry for you? I don't believe it!' she said scornfully. 'Not for a minute. Not someone like Simon!'

'You're right,' Meg agreed cheerfully. 'For once, you're absolutely right, Carol. He thought I was stupid, just as you do. No, I had only one asset, in his eyes. I was the girl who killed his sister, Barbara Melton Hardwick.'

Carol's cheeks paled. 'Wha-a-at did you say?' she gasped.

'You heard me. He married me for revenge, Carol. And brought me here to punish me. Which he has done, I promise you. He threatened to beat me if I didn't work for him. I tried once to get away, but he brought me back. We're quite isolated here, in case you haven't noticed. Didn't you see me hammering on the window this morning? Or notice that he had locked me in? That's why he's making love to you, Carol,' she added maliciously. 'Because he thinks it will punish me.'

'He hasn't made love to me,' Carol said in a stunned voice. 'At least not yet.'

'But I'm sure he will, if you let him know I know,' Meg said callously. 'He will even offer to take you to Denver with him, if he thinks it will hurt me.'

'I don't believe you! He *does* want me! You're lying, Meg, just trying to get rid of me——'

'Oh, Carol!' Meg's eyes danced with malice. 'You are a fool! Did you really think Simon would be interested in a stupid little nymphet like you? He's quite prepared to hurt you to get at me, except you can't be hurt, can you? Because you are the one who is guilty! It's going to be such fun to see what he does when he learns that you are the girl who had the affair with Tony Hardwick. You know, you deserve everything you are going to get in life, but I don't know whether you'll deserve Simon's rage when he learns the truth!'

Carol stared at her blankly, then slowly, her eyes narrowed thoughtfully. One could almost see the little wheels clicking in her head. 'There's something odd about this. Surely you didn't take the kind of punishment you're talking about without telling him the truth?' She saw Meg's face, and added triumphantly, 'You *did* tell him, didn't you, and he didn't believe you! That's it, isn't it?' She breathed with relief. 'He thought you were lying, trying to incriminate me. And *that's* why he brought me from Miami, because he felt sorry for me! He really rolled out the red carpet! And then, he brought me up here, to punish you.'

'You do happen to be guilty, Carol,' Meg reminded her coldly

'What difference does that make?' Carol asked impatiently. 'So long as Simon doesn't think I'm guilty, it won't hurt me. He doesn't believe you. And thank God I wasn't so drunk I mentioned Tony or the job in Miami. Now that I know I won't ever make the mistake of bringing it up. Thanks, Meg, for wising me up. Now that I understand the whole thing, I know you haven't got a chance with him. I might as well try my luck before someone else gets him. Wish me luck,' she added gaily, as she opened the door to sally through.

Even for someone as self-centred as Carol, her nerve was staggering. 'I don't think I will, Carol,' Meg said steadily.

Carol looked back guiltily. 'No, I guess that was a stupid thing to say,' she said thoughtfully. 'I wish I could let you off the hook, Meg, but you do see, don't you, that now I can't possibly afford to?'

And she pulled the door softly behind her, having forgotten Meg's problems almost as soon as she left the room.

Meg saw that Carol had had a lot of questions answered tonight. She must have been puzzled from the beginning about this marriage. Meg and a glamorous writer with an international reputation! But now she knew why he had married Meg and why she had been brought into the picture, she could proceed with more confidence. And if she was unable to pull it off, she wouldn't write it off as a total loss if she managed to gouge some money and jewels from Simon as the wronged younger sister.

After a while, Meg went to bed, leaving her lamp burning beside the bed. She slept the sleep of exhaustion. Sometime during the night, she awakened. Her light had been turned off, and someone was in bed with her. She knew that body, those arms, those hands. He had pulled her against him, and was running his hands lightly, possessively over her arms and breasts. She reacted instantly, hurtling herself to the other side of the bed, confronting him with spitting fury.

'Get away from me!' she hissed. 'Don't touch me!'

'Oh, so we're back to that again, are we?' he asked amusedly. 'Come back to my arms, little cat. I won't make love if you're ill. I just want to hold you.'

'I don't want you to hold me! Go back to Carol! How dare you come to my arms from hers?' she choked.

He laughed and reached for her. 'Don't tell me you're jealous?' he teased.

It was the laughter that did it. Meg exploded with rage, throwing herself at him, pounding and pummelling him with her fists, even biting him at one point.

'What the hell?' Simon grunted as she landed a particularly hard blow in his stomach. 'Why, you little she-devil!'

THE WINTER HEART

His rage flared from hers, but as hers was violent, his was cold, and deadly. He made no attempt to withhold his strength in the method he used to subdue her, and by the time he had finished, she was flat on her back, powerless to move or speak.

'Now, I'm going to release my hands slowly,' he said grimly, 'and allow you to speak, but it had better not be above a whisper. Tell me what the hell this is all about.'

He released the strangling grip he had on her mouth and it took her a couple of moments to moisten her lips and speak.

'I don't want you to touch me,' she finally rasped. 'I can't help it. You are destroying me, can't you see that? If you wanted revenge, you've got it—a thousandfold, but I'm begging you to give it up now. I can't live like this any longer. You're going to have to let me go.'

His hands loosened and she was able to move slightly. He appeared to have listened to her, too, although he still retained her within the circle of his arms. His hands began to rub her back comfortingly, as he said quietly, 'We'll have to talk about this after Carol leaves.'

'No!' she sobbed. She was shivering beneath his hands and the tears were starting down her cheeks. 'It won't make any difference, don't you see? This is the sort of soulless thing I'm talking about. You can't make love to Carol and then come to me. I just can't take this sort of thing any longer——'

'I haven't been making love to Carol.'

'I'm sorry!' she gasped. 'But I don't believe you. It's killing me. I have to get away.' Her voice rose hysterically, and she clapped a hand over her mouth, her eyes demented. She began to shake.

He removed his hands altogether. 'Hush, hush,' he soothed. 'I see you're in no condition to talk about it tonight. Carol is leaving in the morning. I've already called Sam to pick her up.' He moved. 'I'll leave you now because I think you'd rather sleep alone.'

'Yes, please,' she whispered like an exhausted child.

'Tomorrow we'll talk. That's a promise.' The grim vow struck fresh terror in her heart.

After he left, Meg gave way to quiet despair. Why was Carol leaving? Was it possibly because she intended to wait for him in Denver? And was Simon keeping her here because he was more firmly convinced than ever that she should be punished? Try as she might, Meg could not see any other reason.

The next morning, Carol came in to say goodbye. Meg was stripping the bed and gathering up the dirty laundry, when she looked up to see Carol, sexily dressed in a pair of tight fitting jeans, a clinging shirt, and a pair of high-heeled cowboy boots, watching her. With her artfully arranged curls, her inch-long eyelashes and her smooth new make-up, Carol looked as cold and hard and brittle as a piece of glass.

'I'm leaving, Meg.'

Meg looked at her more closely. Carol had lost that budding beauty look. There were bruises beneath her eyes, and she might have been a woman twice her age.

'Is this what you want?'

Carol shrugged. 'Yeah. This place is getting on my nerves. Simon called Sam for me last night.'

'Yes, I know.'

'So you've talked to him?' Carol asked sharply. 'What did he tell you?'

'Oh, don't worry, we didn't talk about the Hardwicks,' Meg said bitterly. 'Your secret is still safe. I didn't even ask him how you managed to persuade him to let you go back tomorrow.'

Carol's lids drooped, veiling her eyes. 'Oh, Simon and I understand each other. He knows this isn't my scene and he was willing to finance my way out. You know, you really are a fool, Meg,' she added thoughtfully. 'You're simply incapable of using what you've got. You should be married to some little guy in a nine-to-five job who brings you home his paycheque each week, and leave Simon to the big girls who know what he needs.'

'Like you, I suppose?' Meg asked sardonically.

'Not me,' Carol said nonchalantly. 'I've changed my mind about him. It's too dangerous—he might learn about Tony. I think you've had a rough time, though, even though you're too dumb to cash in on your situation.'

'So we're back to that again, are we?' Meg felt tired and jaded. 'What do you want of me, anyway, Carol?'

'Do you have any money?'

'Money?' Meg was astonished. 'Your arrogance amazes me, Carol Smith! I'll need every cent of the money I have when I leave Simon!'

Carol looked at her in frank astonishment. 'Then—you're leaving him?'

'Let's just say we'll be parting,' Meg replied drily. 'And unlike you, I won't try to shake him down for the money when that time comes.'

Carol stared at her unblinkingly, her hard eyes momentarily puzzled. 'Oh.' She strolled over idly towards Meg's dresser and began to play idly with her hairbrush. 'Obviously, you and Simon haven't got around to discussing this?' she added thoughtfully.

'No. Nor are we likely to if I can get out of here first.'

'Really?' Carol's back was towards Meg but she was watching her closely in the mirror. 'I wish that I could help you.'

'Do you?' Suddenly, Meg was sick of the whole mess. Yesterday's numbness had departed, leaving in its wake the power to feel again. The pain was beginning to tear at her, hurt unbearably, and she shuddered away from the thought of Simon telling her he wanted her out of his life. Better not to ever hear the words, then she wouldn't have to remember them afterwards. 'If you really mean that,' she said tiredly, 'then you will keep Simon and Sam outside, talking as long as possible.'

'Why?' Carol asked alertly. 'What are you going to do?'

'I'm going to try to get away, of course. Simon keeps our skis in the downstairs wardrobe.'

Carol looked awed. 'Won't that be dangerous?' she asked slowly.

Meg shrugged. 'Probably.'

A variety of expressions crossed Carol's face as she stared thoughtfully at Meg. 'I really ought to tell him what you're going to do if it's dangerous.'

'I have no intention of bribing you, Carol, if that's what you want,' Meg said remotely. 'Don't help me if you like but it seems to me that it's the least you can do, under the circumstances.'

'I guess so,' Carol said cheerfully. 'And it would serve Simon right if you did leave him, wouldn't it?'

'He wouldn't like it. He would prefer dismissing me.'

'Then I'll do it. I owe it to you, Meg,' Carol added generously.

'Thanks,' Meg said drily.

She had no opportunity to be alone with Simon that morning, although he tried to corner her several times. But she was always too busy—putting a load into the washing machine, doing the dishes—until finally, he gave up in frustration.

'You'd better stay in bed until Carol leaves. You're still pale.'

'I'm fine,' she assured him.

She was. The nausea, which she kept at bay through sheer determination, had not returned. As soon as she could, she ran up to her room and packed hurriedly, using a squashy shoulder bag in which to pack her money, her quilting and as many necessary items of clothing as she could stuff into it. Then, dressed in her warmest clothing, she stood at the window and waited.

THE WINTER HEART 151

She had every intention of skiing down the mountain road. She thought she had enough skill to try. But when she saw the smoke below, and realised that Chris was still there, she felt as though a weight had been lifted.

CHAPTER TWELVE

SHE was still standing at the window, dressed for flight, when she heard the whine of the snowmobile. Then the little car with its flashy racing stripe whipped past the front door and around to the back of the house. Meg couldn't believe it. It was an astounding piece of luck. Now, she had a better chance of getting away. She heard Simon call to Carol and, after an interval of time while Carol continued to fuss in her room, Meg heard her footsteps go past slowly and down the stairs. A moment later, the back door slammed.

Now, if only Simon had left the front door unlocked, or the keys available somewhere, Meg thought, as she raced down the stairs. She found them in the back door, dangling.

From the kitchen window, she saw Simon and Carol approaching the snowmobile. They seemed to be arguing. Then, suddenly he turned, and Meg caught a glimpse of savage anger on his face before he ordered Carol back to the house. She must have remonstrated, for he gripped her arms and shoved her along with him, violently. Meg backed away from the window slowly. Something had gone wrong. For once, Carol's persuasive methods weren't working.

She hurried to the front door, unlocked it, and slung her satchel across her back before gathering her skis and poles and leaving. Things went much better than she had ever dreamed they would. The snow had formed a hard crust so that skiing was easy. The only difficulty was in braking at the zigzags but by calling upon all the knowledge Simon had taught her, she was able to perform even that feat with passable skill. When the road widened to include the A-frame house, she slid right up to the front door, where the snowmobile was parked. Chris was bent over it, putting something in it.

'Hullo, there!'

He jumped, jerking out a four-letter expletive, and whirled around. 'Good grief, it's you! Or is it?' He peered closer.

She pulled off her ski mask and tried to smile brightly. 'It is. What are you doing?'

'Getting ready to leave. Five minutes more and you wouldn't have found me here.' She stared, stunned by the sheer coincidence of it. 'Why? Did you come to visit me? How is your husband going to like that?'

'I've come to ask you for a ride. See, I'm all ready to go.' She indicated the satchel slung across her back.

'Not again?' he asked uneasily.

'It's "not again". I always meant to leave, if I could. I didn't have much control over what happened last time, if you remember. Will you take me?'

'I don't like it. I don't want to get mixed up in your quarrel with Egan.'

'It's not a quarrel. It's a war. And I need help badly. Please, Chris.'

He glanced at her, then away. 'Won't he follow us?'

'Given any kind of luck, he won't miss me for a while. There are guests up there—you may have heard the snowmobile a while ago?'

'Yes, I did.'

'He won't start looking for me until they leave.' Meg spoke optimistically, although she had no assurance that she was telling the truth. 'Well? Don't tell me you're afraid of him?'

It was the right approach for Chris immediately felt compelled to defend his courage. 'Who, me? Afraid? It's just that I don't like to get caught between a husband and his wife, but——' He hesitated. 'Oh, all right, come on, then. I'll take you.'

He tossed her skis on to the porch then climbed into the snowmobile. Meg crawled in hastily beside him. He wasn't wasting much time, she was thankful to see. Less than an hour later, they were in Brennan's Pass, where Chris turned in the snowmobile at the rental place and picked up his car—a green Mustang.

In his own car, he obviously felt more secure for Meg saw that he kept a steady seventy and a wary eye out for the highway patrol. They didn't talk much, for they were both nervous and Meg wasn't sure if she would be followed or not. Once Simon realised what had happened, and when he found her skis on the porch, he might be relieved. No, he *would* be relieved, she corrected herself—he wasn't heartless. But whether he would care enough to follow her, she didn't know. Unless, of course, he was angry. Then, he would vindictively follow her to the ends of the earth.

They arrived at the outskirts of Denver about three o'clock, and both of them began to relax. Meg knew it was easy to lose oneself in a big city, and she knew just how to do it. The sight of the flashing motel signs had given her an idea.

'Just pull up into the parking lot of one of the big ones and drop me off,' she told Chris.

Chris pulled into the parking lot of the big motel. 'What are you going to do?' he asked anxiously. Apparently, he hadn't expected their friendship to end this way. 'Do you mean I'm not going to see you again?'

'It's best, Chris.' She patted his hand lightly as she opened the door. He was a nice boy, but he was a direct link to Simon and she couldn't afford to keep the lines of communication open in case Simon had him watched.

As soon as his car had disappeared, Meg hailed a taxi and had it drive her to another motel a couple of miles further on, a small, privately owned one with a blinky sign and a faded triple A rating. Inside the tiny office, she went right to the point.

'Can you let me have a room for one night? Your cheapest one, please.'

The woman at the desk, who may have been the owner, or his wife, looked at her shrewdly. 'I tell you what, dearie, seeing it's out of season and all, I can let you have a single for four dollars.'

'Thank you.' Meg signed the register as Mary Stowe but something about the way she hesitated before putting her name down must have struck the woman as odd, for she added frankly, 'You're not running away from someone, are you, love?'

Meg met her eyes squarely. 'My husband,' she said drily.

'Oh! Well, don't worry. No one but the police gets a look at *my* book, and so long as it isn't a police matter, you're safe with *me*!'

'No police. This is purely a—a domestic quarrel between us.'

'You can't tell me anything about husbands!' the woman observed sagely.

Meg had turned aside to buy a couple of packages of crackers, then withdrew a frayed ten dollar bill from her hip pocket. Something about her pale cheeks and the single bill must have struck a note of sympathy, for the woman added, 'There's coffee in the room, love, and if you want more, just come up here to the desk and I'll leave word for someone to give it to you.'

'Thank you,' Meg told her again gratefully.

Meg dined that night on crackers and coffee, putting aside some for breakfast the next morning. She had already decided that she must proceed as though Simon would make a serious search for her. If he did, he would put Selby on it, and Selby was good at his job. He was quite capable of tracking her down to this motel, but not immediately. As for the planes and buses, Simon had probably 'phoned ahead to Selby and he had had those covered before she even arrived in Denver.

She had to lie low for a couple of weeks, until Simon got tired of looking for her. She couldn't even contact Helen, for it was possible he would spin a tale there that would gain her sympathy. And in all this big city, there wasn't a soul except perhaps the motel woman out there who could give her any advice. Sitting on the side of the bed, sipping her coffee, Meg's eyes strayed to the 'phone book on the shelf. There *was* one name, one point of reference. The art teacher. She remembered his name because it was different. Stanislaus Zarawoski. She picked up the 'phone book and ran through the Z's, then homed in on it like a pigeon.

A motherly looking woman with white hair opened the door to her knock the next morning. The faded, shabby, big house in an old section of the city had been a surprise: Meg had expected Alex's friend to have a modern apartment with cubist furniture and abstracts. But the woman's rosy little face was kind as she listened to Meg's question.

'You've come on the wrong day if you expected to catch Stan here, love,' she said comfortably. 'He has classes on Wednesdays.' She started to close the door, then was halted by the look on Meg's face. She paused. 'Would you like to come in and have a cup of coffee? You look frozen.'

She must be Zarawoski's mother, Meg decided, as she followed her down a dark hallway and into a large, airy country kitchen. It was filled with plants and comfortable wicker furniture with brightly patterned cushions. A couple of skylights and a lot of windows provided the light. And on the wall, unless she was mistaken, there was a Stanley Maynard. An extremely fine Stanley Maynard. Meg hated to stare, but it was hard not to at a valuable painting that any museum would have been glad to have. There were a couple of other paintings that Meg would have liked to study, too, but by that time, Mrs Zarawoski had waved her into a chair and was pouring coffee.

She watched as Meg eased the strap of her satchel off her aching shoulder. 'Oh, my dear, surely you haven't been hitch-hiking?'

'No, I'm not that foolish,' Meg said ruefully. 'It's just that I haven't found a place to live yet. I stayed in a motel last night, but I can't afford that for long.' She reached for her coffee, unaware of the bright eyes that observed the wedding ring gleaming palely on her finger. 'My former art teacher, Alex Langford, suggested that I look up Mr Zarawoski. He—Alex—said he would write to him——'

'I remember Alex very well. Stan always thought him one of his most promising pupils, but Alex, as you know, is lazy. I suppose he hasn't changed? Has he exhibited yet?' Meg shook her head, fascinated by this insight into the character of the languid Mr Langford. 'Stan didn't mention getting a letter from Alex.'

'Are you his—Stan's—mother?'

The blue eyes twinkled. 'It's easy to see Alex didn't tell you much about Stan, did he? I'm not his mother. I'm his wife.' She cut short Meg's embarrassed apologies. 'Alex may not have realised it, but Stan isn't taking any new pupils now. He had to call a halt. His classes had grown too large and demanded too much of his time. He teaches only two days a week, Wednesdays and Thursdays. The rest of his time, he spends in his studio. One of the reasons he bought this house was because of the skylight on the third floor. That's where Stan works.' She waved at the Stanley Maynard on the wall. Meg's jaw dropped, and Mrs Zarawoski laughed. 'Obviously, that was something else Alex didn't tell you. Well, no wonder you assumed he'd be taking new pupils. But Stan has been cutting back on the size of his classes for years. Alex must think a lot of your talent, if he thought you would interest Stan.'

Now, Meg understood. Alex, knowing who she was marrying, thought she could easily afford the exhorbitant fees Stanley Maynard would command. She fumbled embarrassedly with her satchel. 'I didn't know,' she faltered. 'I wouldn't have wasted your time if I had. Of course, everyone knows Stanley Maynard b-but I——' She stopped, swallowing. 'I could never afford him as a teacher. I'd better leave.' She stood up abruptly. 'If you could just tell—i-if——' She halted as the floor swayed. Then, the next thing she knew, the floor came up to meet her.

She came to lying on the kitchen floor, her face wet. Mrs Zarawoski was kneeling beside her, a dripping dish towel in her hands.

'Now, you just lie still until you feel like sitting up, then lie down on that sofa with your feet up. You went out like a light, you know, and all I could think of was that I didn't know who you were or whom to notify.'

'My name is Meg—Somers—and you could have notified Alex Langford as well as anybody else in the world, I guess.' Meg sat up stiffly and moved to the sofa, where she lay back against the cushions and tried to control her swimming head. She had no idea of how pale she was, or how the dark circles under her eyes stood out in prominent relief against the white transparent skin. 'I don't know what made me faint, Mrs Zarawoski,' she went on apologetically. 'I'll be better in a minute, I promise you.'

'I'm not pushing you to leave. In fact, you aren't going anywhere until you have some food.' Mrs Zarawoski was opening soup and putting it on the stove. 'As for what made you faint, it's you modern girls with your ideas of dieting. And my name is Susan, by the way. You may call me that. Mrs Zarawoski is such a mouthful, which is why Stan goes by his second

THE WINTER HEART 159

name of Maynard.' She was obviously chattering to relieve Meg's tensions and relax her fears. Meg objected faintly when she saw the effort Susan was making to prepare a tray.

'I haven't been dieting, Susan. Honestly. I—have been ill, but I thought I was over it. A-and, I've had a couple of dizzy spells lately.'

Susan smiled at her. 'It goes along with being pregnant, my dear,' she said serenely.

Meg flushed. 'How—did you guess?'

'Very easily. I have had six girls and the last two are still at home with us. There isn't much you can tell me about girls and having babies I don't already know. Besides, I noticed the wedding ring. It looks new?' she added questioningly.

Meg looked at it ruefully. 'Yes, it's new. Brand new. I thought I'd better continue to wear it—it will keep me from having to make a lot of explanations later when I have the baby. No matter what people might think, the baby will be legitimate, even if its father doesn't want it.'

Susan looked shocked. 'Doesn't want it? Oh, my dear, is that it? He doesn't? Are you sure? Did he tell you so?'

'No, as a matter of fact, he didn't. But he didn't know for sure that I was pregnant. But he doesn't want *me*, Susan, and I'm not going to make this baby a tug-of-war between us. Simon had much rather I'd have an abortion and take care of my problem that way, b-but I *want* this baby, Susan!' She blinked furiously to hold back her tears. 'No baby could be more wanted than this one is! And I can take care of it, too, I know I can. It's just that this—this next year or two—things are going to be rather hard, until I can get on my feet.'

'Tell me how this happened,' Susan demanded, sitting beside her. 'You haven't been married long and you're a beautiful girl. How did you marry a man like that, who would do something like this to you?'

Meg started explaining hesitantly and before long, she was telling Susan everything—everything, that is, but Simon's name. Loyalty kept her from telling that. But she didn't know how much she was giving away when she mentioned that he was a best-selling author and spoke of the mountain his grandfather owned. Susan, who was a native of the state and knew just about everyone of importance in it, had no trouble putting two and two together. She was surprised, but absolutely convinced that somehow or other, Meg had made a dreadful mistake. But she wisely kept silent, and let Meg have a badly needed cry. Finally, Meg came to an exhausted halt, with the sodden remains of a box of tissues beside her.

Susan patted her hand and said briskly, 'Well, now that that's over, it seems to me the first order of business is to find you a place to live. We happen to have a spare room upstairs and if you like, you can stay there until you can find a job and a place of your own. After you've worked a week or two, you'll be better able to make a decision about your future. Right now, you're in no condition to decide on anything.'

It was a common-sense, unemotional suggestion and exactly the right approach Meg needed at the moment. She began to feel better for having shared her troubles with Susan and when the Zarawoski girls came home an hour later, they found their mother and Meg seated at the kitchen table, examining Meg's quilt.

They were nice, uncomplicated girls, several years older than Carol but nowhere near her age in worldly knowledge or experience. Linda was a student nurse and Jenny a college student, and they accepted without question the fact that Meg was to be their house guest for a few weeks.

So did Stanislaus Zarawoski, when he came home. Meg tactfully left them alone while Susan explained the situation to him, and gave him an opportunity to voice his objections, if any. Later, she carefully searched his face for any sign of reservations. He was a big, burly man with a white beard reminiscent of Santa Claus, and he welcomed her kindly and assured her that he wanted her to stay as long as it took for her to find work and another place to live. He also told her that he had heard from Alex, but had, frankly, forgotten all about her when she did not follow up the letter.

'I wouldn't have been able to take you as a pupil, anyway,' he explained apologetically. 'I would have had to hand you over to a colleague of mine.'

'I couldn't afford it now,' Meg said simply.

The next morning, Stan went in to teach his class and, during his coffee break, called Susan.

'I've found your adopted chick a job,' he rumbled. 'There's even an apartment to go along with it if she wants it.'

Meg was stunned at her good luck.

'Stan says it's a job at one of the Western Houses,' Susan explained. 'Considering your interest in crafts—your quilt, for example—it will be something you will enjoy doing. In fact, it couldn't be more perfect! These jobs are highly sought after. Stan must've got busy and pulled some strings!' She laughed. 'Which, if you knew Stan, would make you wonder for he doesn't believe in pulling rank.'

'And an apartment?' Meg marvelled.

'He's mistaken about that,' Susan said quickly. 'There will be a room, with a roommate to go along with it. You see, the Western House chain runs several hostels in the state, each with its own cafeteria. The rooms are offered at a nominal rate to their employees. It's owned by the foundation that runs Western House.' Susan halted, a curiously arrested look on her face as she stared at Meg. Finally, she said absently, 'I wonder how Stan learned about this job.'

'I don't care—I just love him for it!' Meg laughed. 'But please tell me, what *is* Western House?'

'It's the name of a craft shop, one of a series begun by a private charitable foundation to promote the sale of native Western crafts. It was begun quite a few years ago, by a philanthropist who wanted to save the old crafts, just as the Southern Highland Association saved those in the Appalachians. He had a lot of—er—clout and he organised a foundation to actively seek out the people who could teach these things to younger people—things like Indian weaving, pottery, quilting, blankets, jewellery—even whittling. The things the early settlers had to know to live here. Of course, until there was a demand for these things, the Western House craftsmen were supported by the Foundation.' Susan had been talking slowly, as though trying to puzzle out something for herself, but she added more briskly, 'Stan will tell us what happened when he gets here.'

But Stan couldn't tell Meg much more than he already had except that she was to report the next morning to a Western House located in one of the larger shopping malls. The housing, he had been told, went with the job. His manner was so evasive that Meg suspected he had put pressure on someone to get her the job. As Stanley Maynard, he would know the people who ran Western Houses, the people at the top of the Foundation. She just hoped he hadn't bulldozed someone into making the job for her.

The next day, Meg reported for work and learned that this Western House was a jewellery shop, selling beaded Indian jewellery. They also carried a few other related objects. The beaded jewellery was so unique and unusual, however, that it took full precedence over everything else. There were some cheap pieces for sale to satisfy the casual tourist, but there were others, behind the glass case, that were more expensive.

The shop employed three girls with only two in there

except during peak hours. Later, Meg was to be glad she had had a chance to meet the manager first. Anna Tallchief was Indian and lived at home with her family rather than in one of the hostels. She explained that Meg was taking the place of a girl who had received an unexpected promotion and transfer yesterday to another Western House in Colorado City.

'Debby is angry about it,' Anna explained carefully. 'I will tell you first so you will understand why. Tina was her best friend and they were roommates at the hostel, so she blames you for Tina going.'

'I hope s-she—Tina—wasn't unhappy about it,' Meg faltered.

'Oh, no, only Debby. Tina was happy to go.' Anna grinned.

When Debby came in, Meg saw what Anna had meant. The other girl was unattractive, badly dressed and had sullen manners. She made herself deliberately obstructive all morning, and only Anna's soft voice soothed and prevented an open rupture. Meg soon began to wonder if she could continue to work under these circumstances, and she knew she could not share a room with this girl.

She had brought her satchel with her, and when Anna let her leave at noon, she reported in to the hostel, prepared to fight, if necessary, for another roommate. But to her amazement and relief, they gave her one of the VIP suites on the first floor, with its own self-contained kitchen and a private patio.

CHAPTER THIRTEEN

IF Anna had reservations about Tina's sudden transfer, and the events at the hostel, she didn't show it, for which Meg was thankful. Her problems were already great, and growing greater by the day.

Everyone knew she was married, since she wore a wedding ring and called herself Mrs Somers, but before long, everyone was going to know she was pregnant. And Meg shrank from the thought of the innuendos such people as Debby would cast her way. Also, as children weren't allowed at the hostel, she was going to have to eventually change her pleasant, cheap place to live for something else.

The day Meg thought of that, she was surprised. Until then, it had never occurred to her to think of this job or Colorado as anything more than a stopgap until she could get home to Florida. But she realised now she didn't want to leave. She liked it here, and if she could make arrangements for the baby's care, she wanted to stay.

The only drawback, of course, was that it was Simon's city. At first, Meg had looked for Selby around every corner, but with each passing day, she gradually came to the conclusion that Simon was not looking for her. She might even be divorced. Although she didn't know much about the law, she had a vague notion that Simon could obtain a divorce on the grounds of desertion. And there, of course, Selby's testimony would come in. Anyway, in a few months she would visit a lawyer herself and discover what her marital status was.

Her friendship with Anna developed. The girl was a

member of the Navaho tribe and when she saw that Meg was interested, she talked to her about the customs of her people. One day, she slyly slipped a blue bead in Meg's hair. 'It is for luck,' she explained, giggling. 'See?' She showed the one she wore in her own glossy black braids. 'Maybe it is not so lucky, but it never hurts. You never cut your hair?'

'I used to,' Meg admitted, 'but the man I worked for in Florida thought wearing it like this was elegant, and he encouraged me to let it grow. He was a Frenchman.'

'I tell my grandmother about you. She would like to see the girl with the red hair. Please, will you come to have dinner at my house Sunday?'

Meg was flattered, because Anna did not socialise with anyone else at Western House. Debby, for instance, had never been invited to her home.

The following Sunday, Meg had dinner at the Tallchief home and met Anna's family. They were a large, noisy group, with four generations living under the same roof. Besides Anna's parents, there was an old grandmother, and Anna's two older brothers, their wives and assorted offspring, and two younger sisters of Anna's. Meg was soon holding a baby in her lap while two other black-eyed children crowded at her knees, watching her wonderingly. After lunch Meg asked, 'Anna, do you think your grandmother would allow me to paint her portrait?'

'I did not know you paint, Meg. I will ask her.'

The old lady answered briefly and Anna turned to Meg. 'She ask why you want to paint her. She old and ugly and no longer beautiful as she once was.'

'I think she's beautiful! Because of her hands,' she added simply. 'They are not ugly, because they're strong and show she has used them to work hard. And her face is good, too, in spite of the wrinkles. I would like to paint her sitting in the late afternoon sunlight, with her hands folded in her lap.'

When Anna translated, the old lady looked pleased and gave her consent. Meg bought the paints the next day, and began to work for the first time in months. She discovered it all coming back to her. Painting was again the joy and pleasure it had once been. She painted the old grandmother sitting in the late afternoon sunlight, with the flickering shadows from the aspen tree playing across her strong old face, and her hands serenely idle in her lap.

The old lady was very curious and at the end of each day's sitting, would come around to check on the progress of her portrait, chattering all the while in her own language. One day, she lightly placed her hand on Meg's stomach and mimed the action of rocking a baby. Meg was taken aback. If the old lady knew, then Anna knew, yet she had never said a word. She had been trying to hide her thickening waistline with loose sweaters, but obviously, the old woman's sharp eyes had spotted the camouflage.

Meg kept her canvas and paints in Anna's room between sittings and on the last day, when she finished the portrait, she invited everyone in the family in to look at it. When it was dry, she took it to Stan. He looked at it for a long time, then at her.

'Now I know why Alex wanted me to accept you as a pupil,' he said slowly. 'It is because you paint with the heart, Meg, as well as with the eyes. Will you allow me to ask my good friend, David Campbell, to accept you into his class?'

Meg looked at Susan and she nodded. 'All right, Stan,' Meg said.

David Campbell turned out to be a handsome, virile man in his mid-thirties. He was almost as tall as Simon, with personable features and smoothly trimmed dark brown hair and a moustache. Almost from the first, his eyes, lazy and curious, let Meg know that he was attracted to her, but she soon picked up enough gossip from the other students to learn that he was dedicated to *all* women, not just one. He had slept with most of the available women in his classes, and so sensual was his approach, that it was usually at their invitation, in the end.

One night, as she was packing her equipment away, he managed to catch her alone long enough to ask her casually to come home with him for the night. Just as casually, she refused.

He looked slightly surprised. 'I don't go in for commitments until I've known someone for a while,' he explained kindly, as though that was her only objection.

She wanted to say something tart like 'Bully for you!' but merely enquired sweetly, 'In other words, you try the merchandise out first to see if it fits—like a suit of clothes?'

He looked amused. 'Don't you think that's a good idea?'

'If it works for you,' she said coolly. 'As for me, I don't happen to be a suit of clothes. Neither do I go in for one-night try-outs, nor commitments, so far as that goes.'

'Why not?' He sounded frankly astounded.

'I'm married.'

'Yes. I know.' He frowned. 'But I understood you were separated.'

'I may be divorced for all I know, but I don't want to go to bed with you,' Meg replied witheringly. 'Incidentally, you might as well know right now that I'm pregnant.'

He was intrigued. 'With no husband in sight, that's rather unusual.'

She said repressively, 'I want my baby. I expect to have to raise it myself so that means I won't have time for the sort of life you are talking about.'

His frown deepened. 'Are you trying to tell me you never intend to have a man again?'

'I haven't planned that far ahead!' Meg replied frostily. 'But I am telling you that I am saying not to you right now.'

'But my God, what a waste! You're the sexiest woman I've ever seen!'

'I beg your pardon!' She glared at him.

'We have so much to offer each other! I can't believe you're turning me down.'

He sounded genuinely bewildered and Meg found herself see-sawing between exasperation and amusement. Just then, someone came in and he was forced to stop talking. Meg made her escape.

The 'phone was ringing as she walked into her apartment.

'It's a good thing I got your 'phone number from your records. You wouldn't have given it to me, would you?' was his opening remark.

'As a matter of fact—no. David,' she added patiently, 'I'm not interested in what you have to offer.'

'How do you know what I have to offer?' he asked roughly.

'Oh, I know, all right,' she said drily. 'You drew me a diagram.'

'Okay, okay. So you say, but you don't really know. It could be good for us, Meg. I have a feeling I could make you forget that bad marriage of yours. How about it? Just one time and if it's no good, we'll drop the whole thing.'

'David! I mean it, I'm not interested. Now, if you don't mind, I'm rather tired——'

'Hey, wait,' he said quickly. 'I really called you to ask you to go to a party with me tomorrow night. The crowd will be mostly artists and I thought you'd enjoy yourself. How about it?'

'No, thank you.'

'Why not?' he persisted. 'I won't bring up the forbidden subject. It will be strictly an evening with a friend, I promise you.'

THE WINTER HEART

'I can't. I can't afford to buy an evening dress.'

'Oh, you can come in any old thing to this party. I assure you, even jeans will be acceptable. My friends are giving it in their studio apartment and anything goes. Please say you will,' he coaxed. 'I'll have you home early if you like.'

She hesitated. Finally, she asked reluctantly, 'Do I know them?'

He told her the names. The woman was another teacher, whom Meg knew slightly. She suspected the couple had one of those commitments that David wanted to avoid.

'All right,' she finally said.

'Good! I'll pick you up at eight!' he said quickly, before she could change her mind. 'I have a feeling this is going to be a memorable evening.'

'If you mean that the way I think you do, you'd better not bother,' Meg said drily.

'*No!*' he said hastily. 'I—I just meant I'm going to enjoy being with you. I've never been around the motherly type before. Perhaps some of your staunch principles will rub off on me.'

She got off early the next afternoon, and as she dressed for the party, she wondered uneasily what was the matter with her. She had such ambivalent feelings about her pregnancy. She was happy about the baby; she wanted it, yet, why couldn't she go proudly into maternity clothes? Why was she trying to disguise her condition? Why couldn't she have the courage of her convictions?

Was it because she was secretly ashamed of what she was doing to Simon? She was having a baby—his baby—without telling him. She had been so sure it was the right thing to do until recently, when she'd begun to have these doubts.

She rang up Susan on impulse and started the

conversation by casually mentioning the party. To her surprise, Susan reacted emotionally.

'No, no, Meg, please do not allow yourself to be drawn into David Campbell's life! He is the type of man who must try to seduce any woman who interests him. He will attempt to ply you with wine tonight and——'

Meg burst out laughing. 'Oh, Susan, I love that! Ply me with wine, indeed! Surely you don't think I'm that weak?' She giggled. 'Anyway, he's already asked me to sleep with him and I turned him down,' she added breezily.

'This will only make him more determined. You don't know this man, I tell you.'

'I know his type,' Meg said drily. 'I promise you, I'm in no danger at all.'

'How can you be sure?'

'Well, I've told him I'm pregnant, and I think he'll respect that. He still wants me, of course, but he will go more slowly because he respects my "principles",' she added mockingly.

'You've told him about the baby and he still persists?' Susan asked curiously.

'Yes, Why? Don't you think I should have?'

'Not if it will discourage him. But I think you do your husband a great injustice.'

'Susan!'

'You heard me,' Susan said sternly. 'I feel I stand in the place of a mother to you, Meg, and I must speak as a parent. If you can tell David Campbell, shouldn't you also tell your husband?'

There was a silence, then Meg said dazedly, 'Susan, I told you my husband did not want me . . .'

'I know you are a very impulsive young woman and one of the least vain women I've ever seen. I think you owe your husband a chance,' she said uncompromisingly.

Meg didn't answer at once. She felt winded. She had

called Susan for reassurance and got much more than she bargained for. But hadn't Susan answered her question? Finally, she said weakly, 'All right, Susan, I'll think about it.'

'Do that.' Susan was obviously in a mood for plain speaking.

CHAPTER FOURTEEN

IN the end, Meg wore a coffee-coloured cotton skirt and a creamy blouse with deep lace cuffs. Over that went a short-sleeved blouse of chocolate brown. The muted tones made a perfect background for the jewelled collar she was wearing, which combined all the colours and brilliance of a topaz. With Anna's permission, she had raided the shop and wore a sampling of their rings: one to nearly every finger, and a glistening tiger's-eye that hid her wedding band.

David wore jeans and a cowboy shirt, probably to make her feel more comfortable. As he stood beside his car door, waiting for her to get in, his eyes lingered possessively on her mouth and the burnished curls framing her face. Like most women, Meg was blooming during pregnancy, and tonight, she was glowing with the added excitement of a party.

David was especially attentive during the party, remaining close, introducing her to people and seeing that she was taken care of. There were trays of food, with cheese predominating, and wine. Her hosts were artists, he a pianist, she a painter. Every so often, there would be a burst of music from the grand piano in the corner, whereas her friends were inclined to congregate upstairs in a big, bare, paint-spattered room with canvasses stacked around the wall. Overhead, the black skylight glittered with stars.

For a while, Meg had a wonderful time. She was in a party mood, and it had been a long time. People were nice, although it was obvious they thought she belonged to David. Then, in the midst of a laughing remark, she looked up and saw Simon's back. In that moment, her heart stopped beating. Then, the man's head turned and it wasn't Simon, and her heat started again with a slow, agonising thud.

'Meg! What is it?'

She knew she had turned pale. With a muttered excuse, she dived towards the powder room.

When she came back and asked David to take her home, he agreed at once, perhaps because he thought her paleness was connected with her pregnancy. He did not try to talk down her resistance on the way home, as she had half thought he would, but at the door to her apartment, he held her back lightly.

'Don't go in yet. I want to talk to you about something.' She waited warily. 'What do you intend to do when you have to leave this place?'

'Find another.'

'They'll be hard to find. Not many people want a woman with a baby.' He hesitated. 'I have a house with a yard and trees. Would you care to live there?'

'Are you offering to rent me an apartment?' she asked wonderingly.

'I must be expressing myself badly,' he said ruefully. 'I'm asking you to live with me.'

She tried to joke. 'I thought you always tried us out first.'

'That went out the window the first time I saw you,' he said roughly. 'I've wanted to ask you to come and live with me since the beginning. I never had any intention of letting you go after one night.'

Meg was astonished. 'You don't even know me,' she said blankly.

'I knew I'd foul the thing up if I didn't watch it,' he said gloomily. 'I'm in love with you, Meg. I've been crazy, watching you for weeks, waiting until I could make my play. I've always been the one to pick and choose but this time, I was all mixed up. I tried to be cool, because it meant so much to me. But I've never been in love before. And you knocked me for a loop when you told me about the baby. That you wanted it. It sounded so damned beautiful, I just fell in love all over again. After you left, I started 'phoning you every thirty seconds until you answered. I don't know what's the matter with me, but it's all mixed up with you having a baby. I—I want to *protect* you.'

'Dear David, I am very fond of you,' she said gently. 'You seem like a nice man. I think if you'll stop looking on women as toys, you'll find someone whom you can like as well as me. I'm not at all unique, you know. But...'

'I knew there'd be a but somewhere,' he said gloomily.

'But,' she added firmly, 'only one man has the right to protect me—if he wants to. I think I should give him the chance, don't you? He's my husband.'

'You mean you really do have a husband?'

She smiled slightly. 'I think so. If he hasn't divorced me. But he doesn't know about the baby, and I should tell him.'

'Yes, of course,' he agreed reluctantly.

He opened the door with her key, then stood back. 'Will you let me know what your husband says, Meg? If he's the bastard I think he is, I don't want to get out of your life. Okay?' He handed her the key and kissed her lightly on the cheek.

It was still early, not quite twelve o'clock. Meg hesitated, then went over to the 'phone and dialled quickly, before she was tempted to change her mind. She had memorised the number weeks ago, along with Simon's address. As soon as she had dialled, she realised he might be at home with a woman, and she almost hung up. He might even think she was checking on him! Just then, a deep voice spoke in her ear.

'Hello.'

'Simon? It's me—Meg.'

There was utter stillness. The line between them stretched taut and thin, until she had no idea what he was thinking. That he was astonished was obvious, but perhaps he did have another woman there and was cursing her for her interference. She spoke quickly, before he could say anything.

'I won't keep you. I'm not calling long distance or anything b-but I—I had something I wanted to talk to you about. I thought if you didn't mind—I—if you wanted to——' She stopped, swallowing, thinking how stupid she was sounding. 'That is, I think we should talk. If you don't mind. Tomorrow? Could I meet you somewhere tomorrow?'

'Where are you?' he asked, then changed it quickly. 'Are you at home?'

'At home? Y-y-yes . . .'

'I'll be there as soon as I can. Wait for me.' And the line went dead.

She stood there, holding the 'phone in her hand, staring at it. He hadn't asked where 'home' was, but had spoke with the confidence of knowledge. Complete knowledge. That meant that he had known all along where she was. And that changed everything.

She paced the floor, trying to figure out what it all meant. He hadn't bothered to get in touch with her, of course, because he hadn't wanted her. That was obvious. But why, then, had he been so eager to get over here?

She stood before the mirror and stared at herself. Should she remain in party clothes, tell him about David, and pretend that she merely wanted to discuss a divorce? Not tell him anything about the baby? He hadn't sounded vindictive or angry, as he might have done—he had sounded *eager*. She met her eyes in the mirror, filled with confusion and distress. *No!* No matter what this development meant, she would tell him about the baby.

And why pretend about the other? Why play games about David? Nothing had changed. Who was she kidding? Was she hoping to make Simon jealous? What a laugh that was! He was rushing over here for one reason only—he wanted her signature on divorce papers. He might be afraid that she would ask heavy alimony, so he'd waited until *she* asked *him*. Which she'd obliged him by doing.

She shrugged and slipped out of her clothes, easing the tight skirt from around her waist. This was the last time—tomorrow she went into maternity clothes and damn the consequences! In the bathroom, she removed all traces of make-up and brushed her hair. Nothing artificial, no artifice whatsoever. She wasn't doing a Carol act to get her man back. She slipped into a pair of well-worn jeans and a paint-smeared, thigh-length smock that effectively hid the physical changes in her body.

When the doorbell rang, she glanced with disbelief at the clock. She had an accurate idea of where Simon lived, and not even at the speed of light could he have got over here this soon unless he knew the route well— and was terribly anxious. Her mouth tightened but she had herself well in hand as she flung open the door.

The first thing she noticed were the changes. His face was thinner and there were lines, now, particularly around his mouth. Shadows lurked under his eyes and there were threads of silver in his black hair. He was wearing jeans—that hadn't changed. Like hers, they were worn and clung tightly to tautly muscled thighs and the long legs that ended in jogging shoes. The thick, loose sweater was black, its vee neck exposing a dark shadow of chest hair. Looking past him, she saw a long, gleaming Porsche parked at the kerbside, and she could almost see it smoking.

'Come in.' She stood back. 'I'm sorry to have called you so late. It really wasn't necessary for you to hurry over—it was a sort of impulse, really—I could have waited until tomorrow, but it would be Sunday and I thought——' She was chattering like a monkey and she brought herself to an abrupt, compulsive halt. Waving him to a chair, she started towards the kitchen. 'I'm going to make some coffee. I would have had it already made but you——'

'I don't want any coffee.' His deep voice curtly interrupted her mid-sentence.

'Oh.' She turned back. 'Well, I guess you'd better sit down, then.' He still stood, so she sat down first, being careful to smooth her smock down so there were no revealing curves. She sat carefully, with her feet primly together. 'I guess you're wondering why I called you? I—it wasn't to mess things up for you—your life, I mean. Honestly, Simon.' She looked at him earnestly. 'I—it was just that we had to discuss something before—before things went any further. Tonight, I realised I wasn't being fair to you.'

'Shut up.'

'What?'

'I said *shut up!*' He spoke between clenched teeth. 'I have just one thing to ask you and for God's sake, Meg, shut up your babbling and answer me honestly.' He sounded like a man at the end of his endurance. 'Do you love me?'

She stared at him, round-eyed. 'Wh-why do you want to know?' she asked in a small quivering voice.

'You said you loved me once, and I know you meant it then, although you tried to deny it later. But that was nearly three months ago, and a lot of things have happened since then. Maybe you've changed your mind.'

'Simon,' she said carefully, trying to sound reassuring. 'I am not trying to get you back.'

His face twisted. 'Don't you think I know that?' he asked bitterly. 'If you'd wanted me back, you would have called me any time since you left the mountain. You knew my number and I've been at home, hanging around the telephone, practically the whole time, waiting for your call.'

'You—you knew where I lived tonight——' she began, but he broke in.

'Hell! I've known where you were since you hit town with that little bastard, Chris Turner. Well, not immediately, but by the next morning. When I got to the city not long after you, Selby told me he suspected you were at one of the motels along the highway, and by midnight, he had pinpointed which one. Not because the woman told him—in fact, she'd practically threatened to beat him over the head if he tried to look at her register—but there was something about her attitude that made him suspicious. We couldn't do anything that night—one doesn't burst in on guests in motel rooms—but the next morning, Selby tailed you to the Zarawoskis. And from then on, you didn't make a move that I didn't know about.' He was still standing and now he began to pace restlessly about the room, his clenched hands in the pockets of his jeans. Meg sat down slowly, stunned by what he was saying, the revelations he was making. He seemed filled with a violent emotion that he was barely suppressing and Meg found herself shrinking every time he passed her chair. He went on in a hoarse, angry voice. 'By the time Stan got to work the next morning, I was waiting for him in his office. It helped that we already knew one another—we'd served together on some of the same committees, that sort of thing. He was shocked to learn the real name of the fugitive his wife was sheltering.' His mouth twitched faintly, then compressed. 'I had a little trouble gaining his full co-operation, but finally, he was persuaded to call and tell you you were offered a job at Western House, and this apartment.'

'You mean *you* got me the job and—apartment?' she asked faintly. 'How? Why?'

'My grandfather started the idea of Western House and I'm on the Board of Directors,' he explained impatiently. 'As for why—I couldn't have you taking off for parts unknown. If you were here, I could keep up with what you were doing. And I knew, after everything that had happened, I couldn't force myself on you again until you'd had a chance to decide—to think about it—to learn if you really loved me. If it hadn't been for Susan Zarawoski, I'd have probably acted like the damned fool I was, and come over here and yanked you home where you belonged. But she advised me to wait, give you time. Even tonight, when she told me about that smooth, seducing scoundrel you were partying with! And then, it was tonight—after I'd been walking the floor for hours—that you called! At *midnight*!' he added, in a goaded, strangled voice. He glared at her as though he hated her.

Meg's heart, that ordinarily would have been thudding with fear from all the concentrated fury bouncing off the walls, was beating fast with excitement and a slight smile twitched her mouth. Her green eyes began to glow with delight, but she kept them veiled demurely. 'It sounds like Susan has been a mine of information,' she murmured.

'She has,' he said grimly. 'It's been hell having to wait to see if you'd come to me. After the way I treated you——' His face contorted. 'I wouldn't blame you— that has caused me nightmares, Meg, that you wouldn't—won't—forgive me. I abused you, threatened you, mocked your love . . . But I lied when I told you I married you to make you pay for Barbara's death. Perhaps that was the reason I told myself but I knew, even when I said it, that one doesn't marry a woman one hates. I was kidding myself. And I jumped at the chance to take you to bed, using any excuse I could get my hands on. Every time I made you beg, I told myself it was proving that you were incapable of anything but lust, but all the time, I was hungering to hear you say you loved me. By that time, I thought you couldn't be guilty of all the things I believed and as soon as I met Carol, I *knew*. But I wanted her to admit it—to the both of us. God knows I made myself clear enough when I told you to wait at the house until I could get rid of that little bitch. Sam was picking up his wife at the ski lodge where they'd been staying and they were going to put her on the plane for California, until she dropped a remark or two that made me suspicious about what she'd been saying to you.'

A slight flush tinged Meg's cheeks. 'I thought you wanted Carol. Didn't she stay with you here in Denver?'

'*No!*' He swore under his breath, then came back and flung himself into a chair. '*Want* her? That two-timing little slut? Is that what she told you, Meg? Is that why you pulled that disappearing act and put me through the worst twenty-four hours of my life? Until I found those skis, I didn't know if you were dead or alive. Then I realised that young Turner must have still been at the house. I could have throttled the interfering young devil!' He rose and started pacing again. 'I had calmed down some by the time I got to the city and talked to him. But every day that went by and you didn't call me, put me through hell again.'

'If you'd wanted me back, you could have called *me*. Anytime since you left the mountain,' Meg murmured provocatively. 'You knew my number and I've been at home, hanging around the telephone, practically the whole time, waiting for your call.'

He stopped and turned around. 'Yes, but I——' he stopped, something about her words having apparently rung a bell.

'Hanging around, waiting for your call,' Meg repeated softly. The green eyes were luminous as they met his.

He stood absolutely still, a slight flush tinging his cheekbones. Then, he walked over to her slowly and without a word, reached down and lifted her into his arms. 'Does that mean you feel the same way I do?' he breathed huskily.

'I don't know exactly how you feel,' she replied demurely, putting her arms around his neck. 'You've been here at least twenty minutes, talking non-stop and bellowing fire like a wounded bull, but you've yet to mention a word about loving me, although you've talked a lot about how I was supposed to love *you*!'

His grip tightened and a reluctant smile tugged at the corners of the sensual mouth. 'Very well, my little red-headed minx, I shall take you into that bedroom, and if I don't prove to you in there that I'm so crazily in love with you that I've been half out of my mind for months, it won't be for lack of trying. With your permission, of course,' he added ironically.

'Of course.'

'I am going to try and not act like a wounded bull, although on the other hand——' His voice trailed off huskily. By that time, their lips had met in a long, hungry kiss that reaffirmed their craving and longing for one another. Their lips were still clinging as he lowered her to the bed, so that his body followed hers, and he stretched out full length beside her.

The moonlight silvered the objects in the room as it shone through the sheer curtains that draped the long patio windows. It glittered on the bed and touched their bodies as they lay together.

'We have to talk,' she began.

'Yes, I know, my darling,' he groaned against her throat. 'We both have explanations to make, but please, not now.'

He was shakily unbuttoning her smock and she was just as eagerly tugging at his sweater, her hands hungrily rediscovering the broad, hair-roughened muscles of his chest. His movements became frantic, as he stripped off her clothing and just as quickly, divested himself of his own. The most important explanation was soon going to be made, she thought dazedly, and without her having to say a word. Even now, his lips were eagerly seeking the contours of her breasts, and his hand spread possessively across her stomach. He lowered his head and pressed his mouth passionately against the rounded mound.

'You *knew*!' she breathed.

He looked up, his eyes as bright and soft as a summer storm. 'Of course I knew. I suspected and then—Susan told me. It was just one more torment I had to endure—that you might not let me share this with you, either. You thought I didn't want it, didn't you?'

'Yes.'

'God, no!' He shuddered. 'Susan told me. I was horrified that you had misunderstood me. I hadn't meant that at all. A baby would have given me the excuse I was looking for to make our marriage real. A chance to save face, for I already knew damned well that I'd done plenty to be forgiven for. I'd already realised that I had been wrong, that you were telling the truth. And I not only refused to listen to you, but threatened to beat you if you tried to explain!' He groaned as he buried his face against her throat.

'Why didn't you tell me?' she whispered.

'Fear. Pure fear. I was afraid if I admitted I was wrong, and begged you to stay with me, you'd tell me to go to hell. So I was pleased at the idea that you might be pregnant. It made you dependent upon me— or so I thought. It gave me a voice in your future.' His lips nuzzled her throat, unerringly finding the warm, sensitive flesh beneath the ear. 'I love you, Meg. I love you, darling.'

His mouth burned as he sought her lips and her response was gladdened by the realisation that she no longer had to hide her love. They clung together, exchanging rapturous kisses as though they were starving for the taste of each other's lips, their hands mutually exploring bodies that had been too long deprived of contact with the other. And they made love with a sweetness and a fire that had occurred only once before, and almost never occurs unless accompanied by a strong, sacrificial love.

Those other times, he had stipped her bare of all human self-respect and dignity, and it had done things to her soul that had almost destroyed it, but the worst thing was what it had done to him. Now, they cleansed themselves and each other with the shining gift of self. Their lovemaking transcended the mere physical union and went beyond, reaffirming a moral and emotional commitment. Every movement, every sensation, was an aching delight and when they finally lay in one another's arms, sated, their bodies lightly dewed with perspiration, Meg thought she would burst with happiness.

Simon reached down and drew up the blanket, tucking it firmly around them. 'I think milady mentioned that she would like to talk?' he queried lightly.

'Carol?' she murmured the name under her breath, against his throat, but he heard it, and she felt him stiffen slightly.

'Ah, yes, I do need to explain about Carol,' he said grimly. 'I thought I was doing the right thing, bringing her to the mountain, but instead, I almost destroyed us. You see, I'd already had Selby find her in Miami, and bring her here, because I felt sorry for her, and thought you'd callously abandoned her. She'd been here a week, indulging in an orgy of beauty shops and shopping.' His voice was wry. 'That day—after we made love,' he added hesitantly, and Meg didn't have to ask him what day he meant, 'I sent a message to Sam to bring her to us. I knew something had to be resolved and I thought if you were confronted with Carol, I'd somehow get the truth. I already knew I loved you, and I no longer cared about Barbara and Tony, mostly because I thought that somehow, someone had made a mistake.' Meg gave an inarticulate murmur, and kissed his cheek fleetingly. He retaliated by tightening his arms about her. 'All I wanted, at that point, was the truth. But of course, it wasn't so simple. It didn't take me long in Carol's presence to begin to sense that the mistake—and it was a beaut—had been made by me. By then, you were hostile to me, and I got frustrated. I spent the whole afternoon with that empty-headed little fool, trying to get to the bottom of it all, and all I got from you was rejection. And then, that night at dinner, when she completely cleared you, you wouldn't even look at me. You sat there like a zombie. I don't think you even noticed, did you?'

She frowned slightly. 'No. How did she clear me? She was so triumphant later that she had fooled you.'

He shuddered with disgust. 'Hardly,' he said bitterly. 'She told me you had not driven a car since her mother's death. Along with all the other slips she'd made, it came together. I was sick at what I'd done to you and I would have faced her with it at the table, but you got up and left. Afterwards, you wouldn't let me touch you or talk to you.'

'Because—I thought you'd been making love to Carol. She said——'

'I can imagine what she said.' The disgust deepened. 'A more poisonous-minded little bitch I've yet to see! She was totally amoral. She came downstairs that night, I thought, to wash the dishes, but prepared, I swear, to seduce me! I'm afraid I blew up then. I told her what a mean, conniving little tramp I thought she was, and that I wanted her out of the house the next morning! I didn't even want revenge for what she had done—I didn't want to sully our relationship with any more contact with her. And I wanted to protect you from knowing of our blow-up, so instead of telling you what had happened, I left you wide open for some more of her machinations!'

'She told me——' Meg stopped short, remembering just what Carol had inferred. Remembering Carol's pinched look. Carol had set her up, and fool that she was, she had fallen for it. 'How she must have hated me!'

'She hated us both—after that. Before I finally got rid of her for good by putting her on a plane for California, I learned the full extent of the little bitch's twisting from Selby and Sam. Selby said she'd charged about ten thousand dollars to me at the stores—he found packages filled with furs and jewellery left at the motel for her. And Sam said his wife was threatening to leave him if he didn't get rid of her. Some innocent little girl I tried to force you to accept!' His voice filled with bitter self-contempt. 'And I was taken in most of all! Do you know she attempted to make off with your engagement ring? She apparently stole it right from under your nose that last morning!'

Meg thought for a moment. 'Yes, I guess she did,' she admitted ruefully. 'I was so miserable and unhappy that I didn't even notice.'

His arms tightened. 'I still think I did the right thing in sending for her, although she almost destroyed us. Until I met her, I couldn't fully appreciate what your life had been like, living with her. Or how she could force you, through emotional blackmail, to accept the blame for her. That last day, when she realised we knew she'd driven you out of the house and what it meant if you had a misstep—or fell—she really had hysterics. She exposed herself then. Darling,' he added, swiftly, turning to her, his face nakedly revealed in the moonlight, softened with tenderness. 'Will you ever forgive me for putting you through that? For doubting you?'

'How can I blame you? You were conditioned from the start to believe I was guilty. Why should you believe me rather than the police and the reporters? I had confessed my guilt to them, I can't wonder at you finding it so hard to believe me later.'

'I'll never doubt you again, sweetheart.'

She felt him tremble in her arms and for the first time, she realised the power she had over him. His loneliness and need were as great as her own, and she had been too blind to see it.

'We're going on a real honeymoon this time!' he exulted, with a savage tenderness. 'I'm taking you some place where we can be private and lie in the warm sun and make love...'

'I know just the place!' And a thread of delight ran through her voice.

WHAT LIES BEYOND PARADISE?

atching the pulse of a
oman in the Twenties.
A woman with a dream.
man with all his dreams
attered. The search for a
ng-lost father. And the
scovery of love.
Available from 14th
arch 1986. Price £2.50.

V/ORLDWIDE

The Penny Jordan Collection

Two compelling contemporary romances for today's woman by one of our most popular authors.

Tiger Man
"Adoration has always bored me", he announced. Well that was all right with her. She'd never met a man she adored less. But if it wasn't adoration, what was the feeling he aroused in her?

Falcon's Prey
An ordinary English girl marries into a wealthy Arab family. She knows there will be problems. But can love conquer all?

Available from 14th February 1986. Price £1.95.

Mills & Boon

ROMANCE

Next month's romances from Mills & Boon

Each month, you can choose from a world of variety in romance with Mills & Boon. These are the new titles to look out for next month.

RECKLESS Amanda Carpenter
MAN IN THE PARK Emma Darcy
AN UNBREAKABLE BOND Robyn Donald
ONE IN A MILLION Sandra Field
DIPLOMATIC AFFAIR Claire Harrison
POWER POINT Rowan Kirby
DARK BETRAYAL Patricia Lake
NO LONGER A DREAM Carole Mortimer
A SCARLET WOMAN Margaret Pargeter
A LASTING KIND OF LOVE Catherine Spencer
*****BLUEBELLS ON THE HILL** Barbara McMahon
*****RETURN TO FARAWAY** Valerie Parv

Buy them from your usual paperback stockist, or write to: Mills & Boon Reader Service, P.O. Box 236, Thornton Rd, Croydon, Surrey CR9 3RU, England. Readers in South Africa-write to: Mills & Boon Reader Service of Southern Africa, Private Bag X3010, Randburg, 2125.

*These two titles are available *only* from Mills & Boon Reader Service.

Mills & Boon
the rose of romance

SAY IT WITH ROMANCE

Margaret Rome – Pagan Gold
Emma Darcy – The Impossible Woman
Dana James – Rough Waters
Carole Mortimer – Darkness Into Light

Mother's Day is a special day and our pack makes a special gift. Four brand new Mills & Boon romances, attractively packaged for £4.40.
Available from 14th February 1986.

Mills & Boon

Take 4 Exciting Books Absolutely FREE

Love, romance, intrigue... all are captured for you by Mills & Boon's top-selling authors. By becoming a regular reader of Mills & Boon's Romances you can enjoy 6 superb new titles every month plus a whole range of special benefits: your very own personal membership card, a free monthly newsletter packed with recipes, competitions, exclusive book offers and a monthly guide to the stars, plus extra bargain offers and big cash savings.

**AND an Introductory FREE GIFT for YOU.
Turn over the page for details.**

As a special introduction we will send you four exciting Mills & Boon Romances Free and without obligation when you complete and return this coupon.

At the same time we will reserve a subscription to Mills & Boon Reader Service for you. Every month, you will receive 6 of the very latest novels by leading Romantic Fiction authors, delivered direct to your door. You don't pay extra for delivery — postage and packing is always completely Free. There is no obligation or commitment — you can cancel your subscription at any time.

You have nothing to lose and a whole world of romance to gain.

Just fill in and post the coupon today to MILLS & BOON READER SERVICE, FREEPOST, P.O. BOX 236, CROYDON, SURREY CR9 9EL.

Please Note:- READERS IN SOUTH AFRICA write to Mills & Boon, Postbag X3010, Randburg 2125, S. Africa.

FREE BOOKS CERTIFICATE

To: Mills & Boon Reader Service, FREEPOST, P.O. Box 236, Croydon, Surrey CR9 9EL.

Please send me, free and without obligation, four Mills & Boon Romances, and reserve a Reader Service Subscription for me. If I decide to subscribe I shall, from the beginning of the month following my free parcel of books, receive six new books each month for £6.60, post and packing free. If I decide not to subscribe, I shall write to you within 10 days. The free books are mine to keep in any case. I understand that I may cancel my subscription at any time simply by writing to you. I am over 18 years of age.

Please write in BLOCK CAPITALS.

Signature _____

Name _____

Address _____

_____ Post code _____

SEND NO MONEY — TAKE NO RISKS.

Please don't forget to include your Postcode.

Remember, postcodes speed delivery. Offer applies in UK only and is not valid to present subscribers. Mills & Boon reserve the right to exercise discretion in granting membership. If price changes are necessary you will be notified.

Offer expires 31st March 1986.